FEN

FEN

DAISY JOHNSON

Jonathan Cape
London

1 3 5 7 9 10 8 6 4 2

Jonathan Cape, an imprint of Vintage Publishing,
20 Vauxhall Bridge Road,
London SW1V 2SA

Jonathan Cape is part of the Penguin Random House
group of companies whose addresses can be found at
global.penguinrandomhouse.com

Penguin
Random House
UK

First published by Jonathan Cape in 2016

www.vintage-books.co.uk

A CIP catalogue record for this book is available
from the British Library

ISBN 9781910702338

Typeset in India by Thomson Digital Pvt Ltd, Noida, Delhi

Printed and bound by Clays Ltd, St Ives PLC

Penguin Random House is committed to a sustainable future for
our business, our readers and our planet. This book is made
from Forest Stewardship Council® certified paper.

MIX

To Tiffany and Richard
and to
51.7519°N 1.2578°W

CONTENTS

I

II

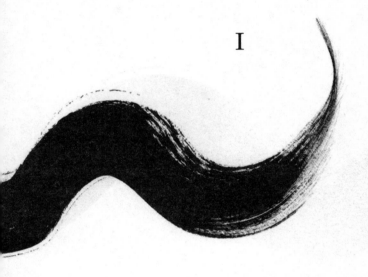

I

STARVER

THE LAND was drained. They caught eels in great wreaths, headless masses in the last puddles, trying to dig into the dirt to hide. They filled vats of water to the brim with them: the eels would feed the workforce brought in to build on the wilderness. There were enough eels to last months; there were enough eels to feed them all for years.

The eels would not eat. They tried them on river rats, sardines, fish food, milk-softened bread, the leftover parts of cows and sheep. It was no good: they reached into the water, scooped them out, slapped them down, slit them lengthwise. There were too many eels and not enough men. And eating eels barely more than bone was not really eating at all.

They burnt the eels they could not eat in piles, stood watching. It was, they were certain, a calling down of something upon the draining. Some said they heard words

3

coming from the ground as the water was pumped away and that was what made the eels do it, starve themselves that way.

We were walking home from St Silvia's when Katy told me she wasn't going to eat any more. She'd stopped in the road. I turned back.

What do you mean?

There were three years between us and I was used to the look she gave me.

I'm stopping eating, she said. I started today.

Even that first night I thought I could see the shift in her. All the lights were on in her room: the lamps on her desk and her bedside table, the overhead, the glow from her computer screen. When she lifted her shirt to change, her spine was a heavy ridge along the middle of her back.

When she wasn't in lunch on Thursday I went to find her. Ducking down to look at feet beneath toilet-cubicle doors, behind the smoking shed; finding her, eventually, on the stile at the bottom of the school field. I'd brought an apple, rubbed it to a shine on my skirt, held it out to her. She was perched on the stile with her knees raised to her chin, not holding on. The fields were half flooded the way they often were.

I said her name but she didn't seem to see me or St Silvia's behind me or anything else until I tossed the apple

4

to her, striking her leg. She almost lost her balance, made a hissing sound, then thumped down and grabbed my wrist.

I continued daily over that week to try and feed her, surprising her with peeled carrots chopped into mouthfuls, chunks of melon, halved avocados. When she ignored them I tried whitely iced doughnuts, chocolate bars, scoops of ice cream. I left the food in places I knew she would find it: on her bedside table, on the top of the cistern in the bathroom, in the drawers where she kept her clothes. I could smell the food rotting in the guttering from my window, did not need to look out to know what was there: doughnuts squashed to jam explosions, browning avocados, a slick stream of leafy raspberry-ripple.

Katy would rap her knuckles on our conjoining walls so I could go and hear how she'd refused biscuits, made clever excuses for missing lunch. At dinner she would kick me under the table so I could observe the ease with which she would appear to be eating. She'd perfected it: talking a lot, chopping everything on her plate once, putting down her knife and fork to talk more, and then chopping everything again and raising up her full fork and putting it down to say something else. Her movements were swift and jerking.

In her bedroom after dinner I watched her scooping food out of the pockets of her blazer, dropping it into the guttering. In a way she'd never done when I tailed her to netball practice or balanced on the edge of the sofa while she and her friends watched films, she included me in this: her starving.

The weekend was easy. We made our own lunches, ate in front of a film on Saturday night, were expected to help ourselves to the chocolate cake, the bananas in the fruit bowl, the freshly squeezed orange juice. She was mutely triumphant whenever I saw her, watching me as I ate two of everything and then rounding her shoulders in an exaggerated gag.

But then, Sunday. Our grandmother. Clipping in on high heels, balancing a mountain of almond meringue in one hand, a pot of cream in the other. The segments of roast came out of the oven one by one. Katy sidling in to watch, holding stiffly onto the back of a chair. The chicken was trussed, brown, cracked, steaming and sliced so legs fell akimbo and the stuffing unfurled. Katy's hands were curled to mounds on the table. She was sweating across her neck, chest and forehead, her mouth open a little as she breathed. She could not keep up her patter at all while we ate, only pushed the food from one side of the plate to the other.

What's wrong with you? Grandmother said when Katy emptied her plate into the bin, refused meringue.

Nothing. Just feel a bit sick.

I opened my mouth to speak; saw Katy's black pupils contracting, her tongue furious against the roof of her mouth.

Go upstairs if you're not hungry.

Katy passed close behind the back of my chair, the bottoms of her feet slapping the tiled floor.

She did not talk to me until after school the next day. Coming up and taking my hand, telling me we'd walk back the field way. She tugged me along. At the top of the stile she hesitated, pale with sharp points of red on her cheeks, knuckles whitening, panting a little. It was over a week now. I wondered what she was running on, air or determination or anger or something or nothing or someone.

We walked along the edge of the cornfield, past the canal and the tree-shadowed dirt where the older kids came to drink; earth dug down into a fire pit at one end, the beer cans, someone's white underwear floating in the beck.

You won't tell anyone, Katy said, not turning back. She took my bag from me, held it over the shorn-back ground. I thought about the sound the combine harvesters made, working through the night. Katy shook her arms so the books and pens and hairgrips fell, scattered. I shrugged, knelt to put everything back in.

You won't tell them, she said.

*   *   *

By the end of the second week she was falling asleep: pillowed on her arms at dinner, curled on a bench at lunchtime, drowsed so deep you had to shake her. I dreaded waking her, seeing her eyes rolling into focus. She missed classes, made me miss them too, grabbed me in corridors so we could go and sit on the stile at the bottom of the field.

At lunch Katy's friends, mobile phones jutting from the waistbands of their skirts, cornered me in the locker room. They were tall, more limb than body.

What's her problem? one of them said. There were streaks of blue highlighter in the girl's pale hair. She hasn't answered any of my phone calls.

She thinks she's better than us, said another, leaning on a locker, jigging her skirt up a notch higher at the waist.

Well. She's coming to Harris Ford's party, I presume, said the first, folding her arms across her ribcage.

I don't know.

They looked at me as if they didn't believe a word.

I dawdled at the end of school, not wanting to pass on their messages or see her falter at the head of the stile, and when I got home she was there already – stood in the middle of the kitchen while Mum moved round and round her, leaning in now and then to shift a strap or move a strand of hair. How could she not see it? The skin on Katy's arms was bleached of colour; her mouth was a stretched line.

Mum lent me her blusher, Katy said, and I could see it, triangular arches on her cheeks. On her neck, the line of foundation was firm. The lids of her eyes darkened with eyeliner, smudging at the corners.

Katy sat in the front of the car and talked and talked. I could see Mum's head nodding up and down. We pulled up outside the house.

I don't want to, I said. Katy and Mum turned round and looked at me and Mum said: what do you mean? And Katy said: nothing.

When we got out Mum leant down and put her face close to mine, pushing the end of her chin and mouth against my cheek, leaving a smear of lip salve.

You OK, Suze? Something wrong?

I looked at Katy. She was on the grass leading up to the house. There was music coming from the open windows and she was dancing.

I looked at Mum and shook my head. Waved at the sound of the car moving away across the loose gravel.

When I went inside I tried to ignore Katy. My friends were there and we sat and watched everyone else. Some of the girls were draping themselves over chairs, lounging with intent. We knew what they were doing: arranging their bodies so their legs were at the best angle, so their faces offered the most flattering side. We would do it too if we had the courage. There were boys at the party, some of whom were at the sixth form college and had car keys

9

and hair on their chins. Mostly the girls didn't talk to them, only turned in their direction as if they were magnets.

In the corner of the room Harris's older brother was holding sway with a beer in one hand and a roll-up cigarette in the other and Katy sat on the arm of his chair. Harris's brother hadn't been to university; worked the mechanics his father owned, had tan lines cut around the edges of his clothes and didn't say much of anything.

I could feel my friends ignoring Katy for my sake and I ignored her too but eventually there was nowhere to look. And eventually she was on his lap.

His hand's up her top, someone said. I didn't need them to tell me.

Later when Katy took Harris's brother into the bedroom and closed the door behind them I knew the whole room was timing their absence. Some people shifted closer, laughing and drinking, trying to hear. My friends and I played fuck, marry, kill; theoretical five minutes in heaven, imaginary spin the bottle. There was a story people always told about a girl who used to go to our school and, they said: lost her virginity to a bike. We marked the outfits round the room out of ten, judged the older boys with what we considered harsh critical notes, talked about our crushes.

Look, one of them said.

Harris's brother opened the door to the bedroom and came forward. He was carrying something in his arms, a blanket or length of piping. Except when he put it down next to me, the head on my lap, it was Katy.

Where are her clothes? There was something in his face I wanted to draw out and strangle. He held onto her hand and then dropped it.

Where are her clothes? I said. I started to take my jumper off, struggling with the arms. A lot of the girls in the room were laughing but I could see one picking up a coat from a bundle and hurrying over.

I looked down at her. Her spine was now a great, solid ridge, rising from the mottled skin of her back; the webbing between her fingers had grown almost past the knuckles and was thickening. Her face had changed too, her nose flattening out, nostrils thinning to lines.

I woke, in the night, on the pull-out hospital bed. Mum was next to me; Dad was asleep on the chair. Katy put her hand around the drip in her arm, tugged it free. We walked along the corridors. With each step Katy made a panting sound. In the bathroom she stood under the shower with her eyes open, her mouth parted to catch the cold water, lip it up. She was, she said, dry as a bone. She stood there until a nurse found us; me curled beneath the sink, watching her.

You'll kill yourself, the doctor said. Katy blew bubbles from the side of her mouth.

In the day they force-fed her. At night we walked along the looping corridors, circling and circling. In the bathroom I listened to the sound of her, coming out red knuckled to stand under the shower, drinking gallons of water so her stomach swelled, mountain-like, out of her ribs.

Her skin was dry like paper, the hair on her head falling out in handfuls. She couldn't walk any more, only hauled herself across the floor, belly down. She could not hear when anybody spoke to her: watched mouths, shook her head. When Mum and Dad weren't there I held up signs for her to read, moving closer and closer until they were a hand's width from her face, and still she squinted, shook her head. Why won't you eat something? I wrote, and she held the paper to her nose, tried to eye each letter at a time, sucked her thick bottom lip into her mouth and then let it go with a pop.

We were in the hospital a week. I sat in the corner of Katy's room and watched how everybody tried not to see what was happening. Though it was clear. It was clearer than ever. Her hands were not fingered now, only heavy unwieldy paddles she used – angrier every day – to knock over trays of food, dislodge her IV.

They kept giving her oxygen. I wanted to tell them it wouldn't work, it was no good. She was drowning in air. At night I brought her bowls of water, lowered her face in, watched the bubbles, saw how she came up just about smiling.

Nights. She rolled out of bed, flopped her way down the corridor on her belly, searching for something. I followed her at a distance. They took to tying her to the bed, straps around her middle, her forehead, her ankles. She ignored our parents, looked blindly for me. I knew what she was asking.

They knew there was nothing they could do for her. We took her home. A nurse would come every day to feed and clean her.

Katy locked herself in the bathroom and would not come out. Sitting on the floor by the door I heard the sound of her in the bath, the water sloshing out, the slap of flesh on plastic, the sound of the shampoo and conditioner bottles falling to the floor. When Mum broke down the door we stood and looked at her but only I would stay, sat on the floor, patting messages through the surface of the water, pushing her under so she could breathe.

The ambulance is on its way, Mum shouted up the stairs. Katy rolled her head to look at me, moving her long body in the water. I wet a towel, lifted her free, carried her out through the back garden, under the hedge and into the field. Her face next to mine, the thrash of her excited stomach against my side, the flapping of gills shuttering on the side of her neck.

I carried her as far as the school field. Paused at the stile to rest. The canal ran deep there, was mired over with weeds and nettles. I lay her on the ground, jerked her free from the towel, pushed her sideways into the water. She did not roll her white belly to message me goodbye or send a final ripple.

Only ducked deep and was gone.

BLOOD RITES

WHEN WE were younger we learnt men the way other people learnt languages or the violin. We did not care for their words, their mouths moving on the television, the sound of them out of radios, the echo chamber of them from telephones and computers. We did not care for their thoughts; they could think on philosophy and literature and science if they wanted, they could grow opinions inside them if they wanted. We did not care for their creed or religion or type; for the choices they made and the ones they missed. We cared only for what they wanted so much it ruined them. Men could pretend they were otherwise, could enact the illusion of self-control, but we knew the running stress of their minds.

We left Paris one morning knowing we would never go back. English was the language of breaking and bending and it would suit our mouths better. None of us would ever fall in love in English. We would be safe from that.

Moving did not suit us; we were out of sync, out of time with ourselves. We rented a big, wrecked house out by the canal. Tampons swelled the drainage system; our palms were crisscrossed with promise scars barely healed before the next one. We promised we would never let it happen again. What had happened in Paris. None of us would let our food ruin our lives. The old walls of the house grew stained, dark swells of rustish wash across the sagging ceilings.

Greta came back most nights mournful; she'd been hunting roadkill. Arabella grew purposeful with unease, raided the butchers and spent the long days cooking up a storm of meat pies, of roasted birds inside birds and thick, heavy, unidentified stews. I was swept along by their disorientation, found myself lying in wait for the large, unafraid mice that populated the kitchen, found myself obsessed with daytime television, endless hours watching old quiz shows or the shopping channel.

We settled. Eventually. Greta, dancing the way she used to, bare feet tapping along the corridors, said it was a stupendous house, a house that knew how to feel. I laid down mouse traps and culled whole colonies in a day. We ate the leftovers of Arabella's cooking obsession in one long, sluggish evening and then emptied everything in the fridge into the bin. There was nothing in there we needed more than what we would have.

16

Arabella invested in a pair of wellington boots, put on one of the mouldy raincoats we'd found in a cupboard and went out on a reconnaissance mission. Came back talking, without pause, on seed-planting schedules and wind direction. She'd been, she said, in the local pub and she'd met men there who she thought would taste like the earth, like potatoes buried until they were done, like roots and tree bark. English men never really said what they were thinking: all that pressure inside, fermenting. We could imagine it easily enough.

She held out her hand, told us to taste it, told us she'd been able to smell their salt-of-the-earth insides across the barren winter fields. We sucked until we could: fen dirt heavy enough to grow new life in it.

Later Arabella broke into seriousness: we would have to be careful, pick carefully. We'd have to share. She changed the Bob Dylan record with her long white toes.

We shaved all the hair off our legs and underarms, plucked until we were smooth, coating the white bathtub in drag lines of dark; moisturised until we shone white and slick through the dim; painted crimson 'yes' markers on our mouths.

We looked the way hunters must do. We looked the way we'd looked in Paris, half-glimpsed shards and shadows of skin, the meaningful line of stocking or bra.

This isn't going to work, Greta said, pulling at her hair.

We raided the backs of the wardrobes; hunted in the dressing-up boxes we'd saved for bored days, snuck out to pillage washing lines. Regrouped and stood silently at the sight of ourselves: jodhpurs and polo necks and gilets.

Greta said, dreamily, that we looked like child catchers.

Arabella said we looked fierce.

She got the money and we pushed into boots and wellingtons at the door and went out, Greta trailing behind to catch her fingers on the blackberry bushes and kick at the frozen puddles. At the door to the pub Arabella turned to look at us for one final check: wiping her thumb at the blood Greta had used to darken her lips, straightening my carefully knotted scarf, mussing her hair with both hands. The Fox and Hound. We went in. Lined up at the bar. Listened to the quiet that spread the way a spool unravelled.

Arabella leant over on both elbows and smiled the way she did and said we would really quite like three gin and tonics if that was all right.

We were hungry but we took our time. Greta liked the school kids, drunk already, though it was barely eight o'clock, and rowdy on it. She bought them drinks because they were too young to do it themselves, laughed at their under-the-table shot taking. We heard her telling them that drinking would only ever get better, that they would spend their lives lying to their doctor about the number of pints they consumed. They looked at her as if she were a thing summoned up, formed from everything they'd never even known they wanted.

Arabella liked the old men in their corners or sat at the bar alone, talking in strange, weathered code to the barman about different ales. She liked the veined alcoholism of them, the implicit watching. She knew enough about the World Cup to get by.

It didn't matter who they liked. The one we would take had raw hands from the cold and narrow, glass-covered eyes. I knew before I went to him the sort of girl he'd want, one shy enough to look as though she shouldn't be there, one quiet enough to look as though she had something to hide. He did not respond in much more than monosyllables to my questions. I liked the dull return of his voice, the way he looked at his glass rather than at my face. He was, he said, a vet. When he was drunker he would tell me it was a bad time to be someone who cared about animals. He told me about the foxes being gassed in their earths. I told him everything has to die somewhere.

I finished my drink and he bought me another, bought one for himself, did not clink the glass I held up, only held his up too: a salute. He spoke about animals as if I knew them too and remembered them well. He worried about the land, thought he would move on when he had half a chance. Less than half.

It's not the way it used to be, he said.

When it was flooded? I said, half joking, and he looked at me as if this were a thing you could not mention, were not allowed to mention.

He was not married, had no children, was on his own the way someone was when they knew no different. I did not ask his name.

We left together. He said he was too drunk to drive and I said I was walking anyway. On the long, straight, dark road I sucked his bottom lip into my mouth and he made a startled sound as if someone had broken something sharp into him. At the onset of headlights coming over the flats I pulled him to the hedge line, forced the gasp from him again. He was afraid of me though not for the reason he should have been. When I took out one breast, he would not touch it, only stood a safe distance and looked until we carried on.

At the house I saw it as he must have done and wondered if he knew what was coming. It smelt of feathers and iron kettles. I took him to the kitchen. There were broken wine glasses on the table; our discarded clothes were in piles. The fur hat on the draining board looked sentinel, only dozing. I made him a whisky and water strong enough he puffed his cheeks out, shook his head.

He seemed unsurprised to find them in the sitting room, dressed in their nighties, Greta's head on Arabella's lap, a Leonard Cohen vinyl turning slowly next to them. I sat close enough to him on the sofa I could see the ice in his glass shaking. He sat and looked around at the rows of records, the 1965 Van Hurst guitar taken from a travelling musician, the signed January Hargrave posters.

Are you in a band? he asked. Arabella called him a lovely man and offered him her hand to kiss. Greta laughed like a child, told him we were groupies and – because she'd been hungry the longest – she got the first try. We asked her if he had the flavour of love and she only smiled a scarlet smile and said he tasted the way burrowing into the earth, mouth whaling open, would taste.

It was not the occasion for leftovers. We buried the little that was left in the big back garden, toasted our success with a whole bottle of something local Arabella had stolen. There wasn't enough of him remaining to merit a burning, though I think that would have been best: a sacrificial fire to warn the rest of our coming.

The next day we woke with a strangeness inside us we could not identify. Tried to stave it off with our favourite songs, our best dresses, opened all the windows to air the house through.

I feel – Greta started to say and Arabella gave her a look good and hard enough to silence her. Said: I'll paint your nails.

I lay watching them. I felt heavy, ached through. Not full – rather bored, weary.

I feel – Greta started again.

Stop it, Greta, Arabella said. It's fine.

I sat up, rigid. I did not know where it had come from but there were things I wanted to tell them right now;

there were things they needed to know. About the giving-in the earth was doing, about the dying foxes and the flood water. The globe was comprised of bone and organ, the mandible of the sea, the larynx and thyroid, the scapula and vertebrae that held it all together. I bit my tongue until the feeling passed.

It was not the first time we'd eaten something we shouldn't.

For a week or so the vet pressed out from inside us. I caught Arabella in the kitchen, weeping over a plucked chicken. Greta began speaking in clipped monosyllables. I caught myself counting the bones in their bodies.

Still, soon we were hungry again. Arabella said that we needed to be careful; this was not Paris. She took up cooking once more and we ate well and often. Sometimes she went to the butchers, came back with quails and woodcock and whole pigs. Mostly she went hunting in the thin spinneys that separated the farms, came back with rabbits and pheasants. Then we got bored of this and we did not eat at all.

When the time came we decided we could not risk picking up another man in the pub. We made a profile on some dating websites, spent long evenings sitting around the computer, pushing one another's hands away. We found a man who, in his picture, showed only his chest, one hand holding up a phone to take the photo. His profile said that he enjoyed drinking and working out.

He wrote that he'd been a sailor but didn't do that any more.

Men like that, Arabella said, no one is ever surprised when they go missing.

We sent him a message and he replied quickly. He used the words cock and cunt and fuck and hard with a regularity which dried them meaningless. Occasionally he'd, typing drunk perhaps, talk about a girl and a baby and a twin brother and how he'd lost the lot of them. The next day he'd regain his composure, write that he wanted to do this to us and he wanted us to do that to him. And when we were done he was going to do this. We said all right, sent him photos of Greta in her underwear, arranged an evening for him to come to the house.

We dressed Greta. This was not the occasion for polo shirts or wellington boots. We painted her mouth a red church.

When the doorbell went, Greta climbed into her heels. The smell of aftershave was palpable through the door. He looked older than he'd said on the Internet, thin at the cheeks, dressed up the way someone pretending to be younger might do. He looked her up and down with a slowness, said his name was Marco and he was ready. Greta giggled. Stepped backwards to let him in. The big hallway was dark. He stumbled on something, an abandoned book or rolling wine bottle. Greta led the way to the kitchen. We closed the front door behind him.

*   *   *

23

The next day the feeling that had come after the vet was back and worse. Arabella went out to get rid of the car. Greta and I sat in silence in the sitting room. Arabella must have been thinking about it on the drive: it's because we haven't eaten for a while, she said as she marched in, tracking mud. We're just full.

We took turns in the bath. The nail varnish Arabella was using to paint her nails overturned, spilt a thin blue splash over the wooden floor.

Fucking Jesus, Arabella said matter-of-factly and then looked around as if to see where the words had come from. Greta laughed and then fell silent, dipping her head beneath the water line.

When I woke that night Arabella was shifting beneath the heavy blanket, her hands doing fast work out of sight, her eyes on the revealed white of Greta's shoulder and neck. I lay and watched her until she turned to me, poked out a concentrating tongue, said: I'd like a piece of that. I want a piece of that. Roared when I reached out to pinch the skin on her arm, called me words I did not think I knew: except, then, I did.

At breakfast I tried to confront them. Arabella was buttering her toast with violent, angry motions.

I think they are inside us, I said.

What do you mean? What the fuck do you mean? Arabella's knife went through her toast and squealed over the plate.

Greta looked a little pained across from me. I wondered if perhaps she was not quite lost yet, if there were syllables she retained that were still her own; if she felt, at times, her own language pressing back.

You're both talking like that boy we ate the other night, I said. The rude one.

Bollocks, Arabella said. Greta got up and went and turned the radio on loud.

I wanted to tell them I knew the truth. The truth was fen men were not the same as the men we'd had before. They lingered in you the way a bad smell did; their language stayed with you.

I locked myself in the pantry, waited to see if I could feel it coming before it got there. I watched out for hints of violence in words that came to mind. I hunted for a thickness in the sentences that formed silently. I was looking so hard for the man that I did not see his predecessor climbing up in my belly again until it was too late.

There was the smell of spice and meat. I dozed off on the warm floorboards, dreamt I was swimming from the inside of one animal to another, moving organs aside with my hands. Often, as I passed from the gut of a horse to one of a dog to a small, angry cat, I could see the sickness beating in them, reached out with my fingers to try and fend it away. It was not until I woke up, Greta banging on the door with both hands and asking what the fuck was I doing she needed to eat some fucking food, that I realised I knew the names for the parts of all the animals I'd dreamt of. It was not a light knowledge, not a thing I could carry with me without noticing or caring any: it was rock heavy, a heated weight. I opened my mouth and heard the words spilling out in a stream I could not see the end of: adre nal, abdominal, abrin, antipyretic, aortic, arrhythmia –

A BRUISE THE SHAPE
AND SIZE OF A DOOR HANDLE

WHEN SALMA was nine her mother died and she went to live with the father she knew only through birthday phone calls and from her mother's steel-lined phraseology – he was a bitch on heat; a fucking rabid, no-cock-and-balled pug with more horn than a wolfhound.

They stood in the hallway and looked at one another.

Pick a room, any room, he said.

She took the attic as if it were a birthright, carrying one suitcase up after the other. Life was a making do and she stood on the bed and stretched to place both hands flat on the ceiling, leaving her prints in dust.

Until Salma turned thirteen the house was just a house. It was too big for the two of them, an up-and-down warren of rooms neither of them had the compulsion to fill. She did not have friends to invite round, did not like those girls at school, their careful observations of one another, the way they moved and talked. Sometimes she wondered why her father did not bring back dates, long-legged women filling the house with the smell of bacon and eggs, wearing her father's dressing gown and slippers, their thin lips purple from the cold. She liked to think it was because he could not imagine there being anybody other than her mother. She liked to think he thought of her by the minute, her dark hair wrapped around his fist, her angry words in the crevices of his mouth.

Sometimes she dreamt of doors eyeing out from walls, stairs descending in quiet conversation towards the floor. Sometimes all the cupboards in the kitchen were open.

What do you want? her father said, coming in from the garden with the smell of cigarettes on his fingers. Why are you playing up? He went round the kitchen and closed the cupboard doors one by one.

She shrugged, not knowing quite why she was lying but doing it all the same.

I was looking for cereal.

Give a house half a chance and it'll answer back. Salma got her period in year eight English class. Excused herself. Folded a line of toilet paper into her underwear and ran home across the field, along the road, down the canal. She imagined the blood flooding across her, darkening her grey skirt, climbing her torso to murder the white of her shirt, soaking her cheeks.

The house felt her coming. Before Salma was halfway there – worrying about how she was going to wash her underwear without her father seeing – the house churned from top to bottom, ached across its spine, made a sound that could almost have been: I. I. I. At his desk Salma's father looked up, shook his head, and went back to work.

She took to catching the bus out to the city. If she left at lunchtime she could catch the afternoon film and nobody seemed to notice her missing lessons. Her brain had been almost quiet before, occasional half-formed thoughts that gave her little or no trouble. She could feel something at the back now, working the way a scarab beetle must do.

That year was the year January Hargrave directed her fifth film. They were not on Film4 or the BBC, only late on the channels no one else watched; they kept Salma awake and came to her often when she hadn't meant to think of them. January Hargrave did not do interviews; was the first woman to win the Grace Heart award and was filmed, at the after-party, saying that if men fucked one another every time they were angry there'd be so much less shit in the world. Salma watched the trailer for the new film enough times to know it would be a length of air against the dull iron of living.

She went alone and sat at the back so she could watch who came in. There were girls who were, like her, alone but old enough to come with a glass of wine or a bottle of beer. They sat with their shoes off and their feet up on the chairs in front. They did not read while they waited or look at their phones, only sat and drank, and she wished she knew them or was them.

There were no trailers and when the lights went down someone who smelt of perfume came in loudly and pushed past her legs and sat down a couple of seats away. At the end of the film the girl was standing, an empty beer bottle in each hand. Salma brought her knees up to her chest but the girl just looked at her and after a bit Salma got up and they went out together as if they were friends.

In the lobby they sized one another up. Looked each other up and down, feet to breast, ignoring the face, as if the face was only a thing that had fallen accidentally onto what was really important. Bodies were what mattered.

The girl's hands were flat and wide and she wore heavy rings on almost every finger. Salma had never wanted to bend at the waist and take someone's fingers into her mouth before.

Her name was Margot and the next night they came to see the film again, sat holding tubs of popcorn they did not eat.

I don't care if it's porn for the middle classes, Margot said.

No, said Salma.

Or if only the art cinemas will put it on, and only twice.

Salma shook her head.

It's the truest thing I've ever seen, Margot said entirely without irony and with a knowledge Salma wished she had.

They caught the train back together and at the Fox and Hound Margot knew the pregnant woman behind the bar by name. In the pub Margot said a lot of things about the underground film industry and actresses and then she stopped.

I like cocks, she said, but I'm trying to be bisexual, even if it doesn't take. I think, in this day and age, it's wrong to be straight.

Salma sat there and thought that there must be moments which were the beginnings of ends; that life must be a line of train carriages and she had just reached the jerk at the end of the first one.

As they walked away from the pub Margot took Salma's hand with cold and sincere authority. Salma looked at her hand vanishing into Margot's and thought about the scene in the Hargrave film *Hooking Up* where Matilda Padel invited her friends round to her apartment in Paris to show them the bed she'd had sex in – and she imagined a stretch of rumpled sheets, the imprint of walking hands and feet pressed onto the clean.

They were at the house. She did not think it was a good idea for Margot to go in with her and told her so.

You not sneaked in before? Margot said, eyeing the tall stretch of dirty white with suspicion.

No.

It doesn't matter, Margot said. Let's take the front door. It means we are unashamed of everything we do.

They went up the stairs on the balls of their feet, arms waving for balance. Outside her father's bedroom she put her hand over Margot's mouth, felt her forefinger slip between the wide, uneven lips. The house dreamt what they would do before they did it.

In the morning Salma woke to hands moving across her. She opened her eyes. Behind Margot's rounded shoulder the house had come in close to watch, walls straining, the breach of effort shaking the bed. Margot was busy with a sort of fierce intent, did not notice. Salma closed her eyes.

When it was done Salma lay and thought the house must feel the way she did; that nothing had ever happened this way and nothing ever would again. She was certain she could feel the pressure of it in her hands, a brilliant pulse in her belly.

Weeks went by. She had bite marks on her neck and on her knuckles and on her feet and around each nipple. She saw Margot most days. Hours were swallowed whole, gulleted smooth. Any time Margot was not there she spent in the bath; water hot enough to burn her clean, windows clammed shut around her.

You'll rot away if you stay in there, her father shouted through the door, banging on the wood.

She did not care. Every sound was the sound of Margot's bare feet, shoes tucked into the waistband of her trousers or held in her teeth, monkeying up the drainpipe.

Sometimes they talked about Hargrave films or lay and listened to the soundtracks or argued with strangers on fan sites. Mostly they took each other's clothes off. Margot said – a line Salma was certain was stolen – that it was a form of worshipping. And, yes, there was something church-like in the risen struts of Margot's body, the flesh in between. Something, even, in the slow act of it, secretive enough perhaps it was a thing you would only ever talk about in a confessional.

Salma had read books where couples kissed, spoke in platitudes or come-ons; something about to happen, hinted at. Beyond that there was always only a white space on the page. A gap between paragraphs. She had thought often about what went on there. On the other side, when the letters appeared once more, couples smoked or drank tea or dressed one another or themselves. If there was a book to be written about Margot it should be blank; it would be those sex spaces between lines, sucked clean of words.

* * *

33

Salma wanted, more and more, to tell someone about Margot. Something had happened and it changed the way the fields looked and the way she moved at school. She imagined, on the fen, the flood water was starting to rise back across the flats so it could hear her confess. She felt the heavy words pressing at her mouth – at the till in shops when asked if she needed a bag; at school when Ms Hasin asked them to run round the field. She wanted, one of those girls – even them – to stop her in the corridor and ask if she was 'seeing someone', if there was anyone she thought about more times a day than she thought about herself. She wanted one of them to push her against a locker or trip her going in or out a room and for her to rise up and tell them with pride about the girl she loved. To go up to her father's study and push the door open and stand triumphant.

She had to tell someone. The words scalded her insides. In the end there was only the house. She jammed her mouth close to cracks in the walls or pressed her lips at the openings of taps and whispered about the shape of Margot's feet or the sound of her rings as she washed her hands.

In response? Only silence. But in the morning she would wake with bruises shaped like curtain hooks, half-blind from the detonation of a light bulb into a tiny, pained sun. She would find wall chips in the lasagne, pick shards of glass from the soles of her feet in the morning, walk into suddenly closed doors, trip on the raised ridge of a step. It was a jealous answer.

This is what Margot did to you. At night the house felt it worst: the pipes in the walls gurning, the oven burning through and through the dark, the heat of everything else: radiators and kettles and the airing cupboard. It had seen her going silently, balanced, up the stairs, seen skin coming from beneath clothes.

The house did not love the way a dog would love, unthinking, beating back up after a cuff to the nose; or the way a child did, through lack of choice and necessity. It loved her darkly and greatly and with a huge, gut-swallowing want that killed the hive of wasps that were building hard in the wall and cut the electricity for odd, silent hours: Salma's father humming tunelessly in the attic, torch in hand, fiddling with the fuse box. When the lights came back on, the radio and television and washing machine jerking into action, he raised his hands in mute applause, but it was not him who had done it.

The house did not have the human complication to worry that its love spun often into hate. Or to think that the shape of Margot beneath the blankets, or the rise of mosquito bites as if they were curses on her skin, was not her speaking back, not words or a signal, only an oblivious living.

Margot saw the house's love before Salma did.

Look, she said – look the bloody hell at this.

She yanked Salma's hand away from the book she was holding and pressed it, palm down, against the wall. They were in the attic; the wallpaper bellying down. Margot held her to the spot until Salma cried out and then let go. When she looked at her hand, the palm was red from the heat of the wall. She stepped back, out of reach, her hand wedged beneath her armpit.

Look. Margot was up close to the wall, fingers pressing until the heat became too much and then withdrawing. Returning with insistence, withdrawing.

Come on, Salma said, let's go downstairs.

What do you think it is? Margot dropped her hands and approached the spot with her mouth, tongue out to taste the heat flicker on the air.

Come on, Salma said.

Margot didn't reply.

That night Salma pulled the tool box out from under the sink and laid everything out on the kitchen table for the house to see. She carried the hammer down into the basement and set to against the soft walls. Fell asleep in a cloud of dust, dreamt of power tools. Woke up knowing there was no telling the house; it was not listening.

Pleading with Margot was something you built in layers, worked up with cups of tea and cake and fast-moving hands. She was nervous enough she burnt the bread she was toasting, put milk in Margot's earl grey, cried. Margot went into the sitting room with that hip-sway which told you she was going alone and didn't want to be followed. Salma wanted to tell her she would follow her everywhere, that she was so sick with Margot there was no room inside her for anything else.

She started again: made tea in the pot Margot said was retro, cut slices of cake thin, the way Margot liked them. She prepared her face outside the sitting-room door, went in backwards. Turned with the tray held out: surprise. The music was still on, loud enough to shake the mugs, but Margot was not there. She left the tray on the floor and went looking. In the attic, throwing aside the lumped duvet with a rush of hope. Tracked through the halls, listening. The house moaned a long, low note that Salma felt in her feet and in her teeth.

Margot's clothes were in a pile outside the bathroom door. In Hargrave films cowboy hats were left on door handles and this felt the same: a warning wink. She kicked them aside, walked in. She had never seen Margot naked from a distance before, the body out of tone: the sharp odd protrusions of hard pressing out from soft.

Margot did not look up. Her hands were moving, stroking away at the walls, at herself. The ceiling brushed the back of Salma's head as it pulsed; the walls were soft as egg whites. Margot's mouth was open like a claw. The wall ate up the window with the sound of a bubble breaking; shrank the sink into itself, caught handfuls of Salma's hair and pulled them tight as bungee ropes. Margot's left arm was swallowed to the elbow in something that once was wall and now was loose, flabby. With a dry gasp her legs vanished to the knee. Her right arm was taken at the shoulder. Salma was pushed backwards by the sucking walls, the force of them grubbing forward, filling Margot's mouth. Edged over stomach and breast and neck until Margot was gone.

It was done. The walls shrank back, the sink hardened, the window snapped open onto cold air.

You have to eat, her father said, you have to sleep, you have to get off that sofa and have a bath.

She could not see the logic in this. She dreamt up breakings: foundations gorged under the heft of yellow diggers, walls pulled from each side until torn, doors splintered under fallen pianos. She wished she could not see it: Margot's handprints rising on the skin of the doors; her voice coming from the open oven door, emerging from the taps. The house was filled to the rafters with the smell of what had happened. Her father popped all the windows and bought air fresheners for all the rooms but the smell stayed: rock salt.

Salma brought home boys she found in the pub, in through the attic window, pushing them backwards onto the floor. The house shifted around her like a wound. When the boys orgasmed she lifted her head to hear the sound the house made; a quick exhalation, dust rising in pillows. The house showed its displeasure: her feet bloody, the sound of the boys falling with a whoomph from the drainpipe. The television turned itself on at night and surfed till it found the films Margot had talked and talked about.

HOW TO LOSE IT

1999

NEVER SEEN a man naked before. Clothes coming
apart until – there he was.

Isabel thought she would remember him whole:
standing afterwards at the window checking his messages
or standing at the base of the bed looking down at her.
Instead she kept only bits of him: the slick of snail trail,
the dry skin on his thighs and upper arms, the rake of
spine vanishing at its base.

What was it like? Shields asked her.

Dunno.

What?

I don't know.

Shields looked as though she didn't believe her. Shields
had never seen a man without his get-together on.

But what was *it* like?

Isabel knew what Shields was asking. The bulge of it ribbing out the front of his trousers, the eyeing length of it in flat propulsion against his belly. The probing of it at her thigh line and after when it was leached up and he handed it away out of view.

You know, she said. You know.

Though Shields didn't and she felt nasty for not giving her something to take away. Not even something about the hotel. The blonde kid throwing up in the lobby so no one noticed her going in, taking the stairs. How all the corridors looked much of a muchness and none of the room numbers joined together so she ended up wandering a good distance in the wrong direction. Something about the light in the room when he opened the door; stale light. The window didn't open enough to take even an elbow and with the smell of cigarette butts it needed to.

If there had been a way not to, she probably wouldn't have taken off anything when he told her to. Though on the train she'd wanted it and at family parties when he was the only person she wasn't related to – taking her aside to tell her about Russian literature – she'd wanted it even more. Wanted it bad enough to make all the right motions in the right order and find herself there: down to her pants in a Holiday Inn, return train ticket in her purse to make sure she didn't stay. He called her Fizzy Izzy the way he always did and she, playing the part, grimaced to make him laugh.

Well, you did it, anyway, Shields said, swinging herself down off the car bonnet.

What?

You got rid of it. Didn't you?

Virginity was a half-starved dog you were looking after, wanted to give away as quickly as possible so you could forget it ever existed. The girls at school: whose was worse, whose lasted longest, where it happened, when.

Helena's story. That older college boy, tattoos like handcuffs round his wrists and the bar cutting his eyebrow silver, hanging outside the gate after school, putting his hands up Helena's shirt out where all the parents could see. Helena said she was holding out, said he didn't want it bad enough yet. It was the lingo of sales and stocks; what was the best deal, when was the right time to sell it all.

Isabel saw it in full colour: the shape of the boy's arms as he lifted the garage door, the skirt short enough for Helena to save till then, the bike he wheeled out to her. It was, Helena said – approaching the punchline with eyebrow cocked – a boy's bike. A fucking racing boy's bike, high enough he had to hold the drop handlebars while she climbed on.

What do I do at traffic lights? she said, legs wavering, clutching his shoulder.

His eyes were the colour of skylines, his shrug nonchalant enough to shudder feeling up her thighs, along her belly.

Don't stop, he said.

She set out ahead of him, down the road, skirt snickering high enough to thigh her plan of action to Mrs Waiting's net curtains: she'd lead him out along the canal towpath and down, find a good hedge, be waiting like some knowing nymph when he caught up.

She heard him running behind her, wheeling the bike to gather speed. There was the rattle of the cards fixed to his spokes. She lowered her shoulder to take the turning onto the towpath. The ground pitted deep; the hole she saw ducking beneath her handlebars, the wheel turning as it went in and her pitching forward and down onto the bar between her legs.

So I lost it, Helena said, shook her head with wry impatience at the forecast of everything; of life and what it surely would bring. Virginity lost against the bar of a bike.

Isabel thought often about the traffic lights, imagining Helena and the boy skidding through the reds; not yarring sounds of fear or triumph, but silent in concentration. Even in a hotel room with cigarette-smelling sheets, even with a man twenty years her senior and the only person her father ever got drunk with, even with no condom, she'd thought it would be like riding red lights.

2014

Mrs Williams had not held onto the end of the bunting and now half of it was in the pool, beginning to sink. The other end was cording up into the rafters. Kitty was sat on the stone steps, holding her swimming cap. When Mrs Williams waved at her she went and put her toes over the edge, drafted her body skywards and then arrowed down.

She came up with the bunting wrapped round one fist and towed it to the far end. Tied onto the rafters it hung, dark with water, dripping a little.

Go wait with the others, Kitty Moore. Mrs William shouted as if there was another Kitty there.

She went into the locker room. The swim team were sat around, not doing much, some of them in underwear or fully clothed and wearing their caps. Kitty was cold: turned the shower on and ran it till hot. The walls of the shower room were slick as always, seams of mould running lengthwise down the corners, clogs of hair in the shallow yellow guttering.

Why you wet? someone said. Kitty switched off the shower.

Williams dropped in the bunting.

There was a joke at that but Kitty didn't hear much of it, only laughed when the rest of them did. She was thinking on the night before. All day she'd thought of it, seeing the words pulsing out from people's lips and not quite getting them; stood for a good twenty seconds at the chips-or-mash question in the lunch queue.

Kitty thought her mother should understand that you couldn't have a fifteen-year-old daughter when you were thirty-one without everybody knowing you'd been one of those girls who gave it away fast as a hot potato. And you couldn't expect either, Kitty thought, your daughter not to get old enough to do the maths. All the same, it hadn't meant much until she came back early from school the day before, came in quietly, and heard the sound breaking across everything. She turned on the television, the radio, made the microwave buzz twice reheating curry, let the kettle build up a steam. Still: he came down first. Came right into the kitchen and swung the fridge wide before he saw her at the table.

Shit, he said.

Hi, she said. Hello.

Hi, he said. Hello. Hello.

He was greying in the stubble across his face, his eyebrows and the hair triangled at his bare chest, but his head was dark; like a badger, though he was thin, thinner than her mother.

I'm your mother's friend, he said. Holding the side of the fridge.

OK.

We used to live together.

Right.

We lived on a canal boat.

OK.

He left the fridge and went out and she could hear him calling up the stairs. Isabel, Isabel. Isabel.

It had hung over her all that day. Hung over her enough that when the boy none of them knew poked his head round the corner of the changing-room door, seeing Harriet pretty much without anything on, and let out a low whistle before retreating, it meant more than it ever should have.

She didn't know who he was or care much. Only that nothing could mean nothing that day; the French teacher dropping a cup and breaking it, the hair Kitty found in her mashed potato, the words that came out instead of other words; the writing that was left on the whiteboard.

Mrs Williams came into the changing room and started to yell. Now and then the lights flickered off and then back on again, the girls frozen in the dark to wait, swearing and coughing. Kitty imagined the lights above the pool turned high enough to sap electricity from the whole town.

They lined up in order. She could smell the changing rooms, dank and overused, the chlorine and the sweat under her arms. The others put on their caps, jostled and pushed and laughed. The lights dimmed, dipped, went out again. Between the benches there were slips of nothing space, dimness. When the lights came back on she was certain she saw a shape move, shifting behind the lockers – turned; nothing.

At the head of the line Mrs Williams waved her arms, half salute, half orchestration. When they went out Kitty's mother was there, hands tucked into her armpits, chin lowered. Behind her, almost a silhouette, was the boy from the changing room. He looked the right age to go to their school, looked like he could be good at maths or English and be awkward at school discos. He looked, also, like he could go to the all-boys' school one town along, share a dormitory with five others and hitch-hike to town, make older boys buy him beer. He looked like he could do all those things or like he did none and never had. Seeing her looking, he moved an eyebrow upwards; she was not certain what that meant.

Her race was last. She rounded her toes over the edge, swung her arms. She barely saw the others diving off, knew, even then, what she would do – a sort of answer to the badger-haired man in the kitchen, or a sort of question to the calculations that amounted from her age against her mother's. Or maybe just to do something, just to do anything. Like those older girls in the changing room who said studiously: I only ever date to fill the time.

She was thinking on it hard enough she came near the back though any other time she would have won and any other time she would have cared on losing. She pulled herself out, felt the water coming off in a sheet and moved her head up. Her mother was there, staring at her.

There's a party, Kitty said to her, moving her eyes over the ridge of her shoulder at the boy. I'll see you at home.

She expected her mother to argue. Where's your towel? she said instead.

In the changing room Kitty drew out dressing, talked enough that a sock took ten minutes and most everybody was gone by the time she was ready. Took a book to the toilet and sat with her feet resting on the bin. Sat till the lights were turned off.

When she went out he was there. Sat on a bench, hands hanging down, looking at her. It was easy to hunker down and fill that space between his knees with her body like she knew what she was doing.

Was there something other than hair and eye colour that you got from your parents? The shape of his face inclining down her, over her stomach, down her. Was there something more than a way of thinking and walking, a certain accent and easily angering, the type of tea she had, the amount of sugar? Was there repetition also in events, so that things swung round twice and you barely noticed them until, years later, you heard your story spoken through someone else's mouth?

The feel of someone other than her down there was surprising. Not knowing it was his tongue until she felt his hands higher up. Wondering, not having time to feel any horror at the thought, if this was how it was for her mother; on the floor of a changing room still slick from the showers, still half in clothes, still half out of any real-isation of being there. As if somehow her growing from that moment had grown the moment into her so she could never have been anywhere, other than there. And then the terrible thought that her mother must know what was happening; the cord which trailed through events, spanning time zones, spanning both ways, must be pulling tight.

He was coming back up her body.

You got a condom?

No, she said.

He shrugged. S'okay.

The unlit pool was dark enough you could not tell ground from water and she heard him going in before she'd felt her way to the edge of it. There was an ache at the base of her, a pressing in.

Come on, he said from somewhere.

She bent her knees, fell forwards, closed her eyes. Held her breath for as long as she could, moving her arms beneath the water, frogging her legs out to either side. Waiting for the heated beat in her chest and then pressing her toes flat to the floor and shrugging up.

His slipstream passed under her, fingers leaving a stream of their own across her calves. Then gone. She swam on. He moved under again a moment later, willowing up this time so she felt the entirety of him against her, seal-like, hands making their own way.

I think this is how my mum lost it, she said before she could stop herself, unnerved by how he felt: made more of water than anything else.

He didn't say anything for a moment, then: In a pool?

Yeah. Maybe.

She told you?

No.

His hands were working beneath the water, strict with purpose, his breath very even.

She lived on a canal boat for a bit.

Cool.

It was cold and mouldy and she wouldn't do it again if you paid her, she said. Then she had me.

He didn't say anything.

There were slugs, she said.

The side of the pool against her back was cold, sudden and hard: she grated the skin off and opened her mouth in pain long enough for him to slide a finger in. She thought then, catching it accidently or on purpose between her teeth, that he must be able to see her. That only she was mole-blind in the dark and grasping. He put his hands beneath her thighs and lifted her. She was more than half out of the water, skin rough with cold, his mouth on her, a growing pressure in his hands.

You ready? he said, sliding her down.

She pushed him with both hands, one on his head to better force him, felt him dip beneath the water and, as he did, she rose above him, grasped backwards. His hand held onto her leg for a moment and then was gone. She pulled herself out; the breath as he swam away from her, whistling disappointment or goodbye.

She walked home along the dark road, tracing through the pattern of what would have happened, of what could have happened: the press of him against her, his breathing giving nothing away and nothing away till there was nothing to give. The imaginings of what her mother had done: the canal boat frozen hard to the riverbank, the baby growing and growing: her. She pictured him: the badger-haired man, darkening backwards till he was young, too young to have a baby though there it was, swelling beneath his hands.

Ahead there is a red seed of light, sharp enough to cut through to her. She is uncertain what it is.

1999

Some days they were on the roof till dark, sat in stolen deckchairs, talking about where they would go when they got the motor working. Finn trooped to town for Cornettos, Isabel raised her top to show the white strain of stomach to the weak glazed sun, watched the kohl eyes of swans on the opposite bank, the low skim of willows.

They would take the canal boat to Africa, watch its nose dip-diving sea waves, be unrecognisable by the time they got there, wood-brown skin, hair salted white. Always, in Isabel's imaginings, the baby was with them, a sea cub, a traveller forming a lingo all its own. There wasn't room on the boat for more than a few books but they'd swap them at docks and the baby would puzzle them out, quote them, grow a language only they understood. They would not need anyone else. The baby would be expert at slitting fish so the skeletons fell out fully formed; understand the seasons from a finger to the knuckle in the river; know the tunnels whales took.

Then there were nights she woke and felt the thrum of cold beating through the base of the *Marie Cardona*. Finn curled close for warmth, one hand held against the moonrise of her stomach. In those moments he was barely more than a baby himself: quiet sleeper, breathing content, smooth skinned. She lay there, tallying up what he'd left behind.

Some days she woke to him gone. Stoked the fire. Sat in front of it until it chugged enough heat to bring her body back to her. She would not go up to see if she could sight him. He could leave if he wanted, would come back if he needed.

Later there would be the sound of someone on the towpath, the extension of his body as he came down the green-painted steps towards her, grin saying he knew she'd been waiting.

Where you been?

He wouldn't answer; only flexed his fingers onto the globe of her stomach, murmured words Isabel could not hear, as if he and the foetus had some secret they were growing.

Get off, you. She'd nudge him off balance with the ball of her foot, laugh as he fell, extravagantly.

She would and must forgive him anything because he was there. Waking her some days with the lighting of the fire, scrambling eggs in the one burnt pan they had, filling the silence. Once he came back with a bagful of books. Once, when she said she was craving meat, they ate chicken for a week, and though the sell-by dates told her where he was getting them, she said nothing.

She tried to think of them both sprung fully formed from the walls of the boat: but she sometimes thought of Finn at school. Pitched in with a group of boys. Clever, front of class, arm raised lazily as if offering a favour. Pitching out quotes he'd spent all night learning. He could get marks better than most without much trying. But he did try.

She'd not noticed him much until after the baby was inside her and then she watched him reading, saying phrases out loud to impress her; eating enough for two at lunch and then running it off like a terrier round the field.

She knew what he wanted, though he only ever asked without knowing: the rise of his penis against her leg as he slept, possessive pronouns he used without consideration, his coming there at all. Some days she saw how careful he was, how little he touched her, how he turned away when she undressed or joked forcibly about masturbation or girls at school.

The first time they talked about baby names he said he thought it wouldn't be human when it came and they should take that into consideration.

What? she said, cupping her stomach. What the fuck does that mean?

Finn said he imagined instead, thinking on it, a tiger cub or baby bird or half something and half something else.

Half what and half what? She was more suspicious and aggressive than she meant, as if she thought his words had some sort of power to bring it on. He shrugged, tried her out on homemade beasts for a while until he ran out of animals to mix: horse and squirrel, hamster and eagle, wolf and whale.

She knew what he was saying – that, though they never had, he could not imagine her having sex with anyone other than him. Her not telling him who the foetus's father was only proved to him she never had. She could never be certain how badly he thought these things, how seriously he imagined her that way; virginally surprised on waking to find a swollen stomach, the kick of hoof or paw against her hand.

When winter came she watched their imaginings pick up force, saw how they ballooned up to fill the low-roofed cabin. The baby was coming a fox, mudded brown to start and then reddening out like a firecracker. Wild enough to give them the slip at ports and come home just at the hour of leaving. Kind enough to come with presents tied beneath its chest, swinging round its neck: Moroccan candle-holders, long sticks of incense, bags of spice, live chickens to supply everyday omelettes. Clever enough to sit up with them on quiet sea evenings and debate the spans of evolution, snout narrowing in thought, claw-sharpened fingers tapping.

They would fish on their journey; that's how they would fill their days. Or no, he said, rather they would hunt whales, beach the great bodies onto stony shores, strip their insides, oil the boat with blubber to keep out the cold, make coats from the tough skin, use everything there was and sell nothing, only chip bowls from teeth; make whale soup, whale stews, use tail fins as kitchen shelves.

When she got up to wee she found sheets of frost in the shower, mould climbing further and further up the corners, slugs gathering everywhere in silent conference.

Some days that winter they could barely stand the sight of one another. Stalking round till one or the other gave cause for beginning and then it could be dark before they stopped. She did it with her hands, breaking bowls and cups, tearing pages from books. He said words quiet enough she couldn't hear until she grew still and then he said them again, repeating them syllable for syllable, slow enough she saw the awful ends of the sentences progressing towards her.

By night they were both sorry. She on the sofa, glueing crockery back together. He could not say it to her, only told the foetus he would never say anything like that again. They both knew she would break the plates along their glued lines the next week and he would say the same lines over, word for word.

And it was that winter she realised the danger of the imaginings, but let them come anyway. Said nothing to dissuade him when he first spoke of the children they

55

would have to keep the fox child company. Human children that would come with the tides and have gills as well as lungs, webs between their toes and fingers. The fox child was the clever one but the babies they had together were water from birth, happier swimming alongside than driving the boat, happiest looking up at the sun through the surface. They would spend most of their time missing them.

Sometimes she woke believing it. The cold hard enough to imagine it sea-sung, the smell of them in the same bed like salt, the feel of him well known. Sometimes she woke thinking she had just missed the sound of a fox barking; an easy step from that to believing them older and the sounds of river water really one of their water babies, touching wet pads down on wood. He must, she thought, feel the sudden belief sleep-strung through her. His hands knew anyway.

He picked up a pattern like they were old and still good at it, used his tongue on her like it knew its way.

What's the problem? he said, skidding away across the bed when she stopped him, his back to the wall, not looking at her. What's the problem? You can't get pregnant right now, can you?

Later, outside, there was snow on the fields and on the towpath and the river was iced into concrete lines. He flapped the deckchairs to unstiffen them and they sat looking out over the grey and eating their burnt scrambled eggs.

Looking at him Isabel imagined him older, waking up ten years later on his sofa and knowing how many children he had and the shape of his wife when she slept. This was what he would become. How much coffee did he drink at the weekends, how many glasses of wine did he allow himself? He ran, sometimes, through the park. He made a good carbonara and did not burn eggs.

She could not stop thinking of the traffic lights, of riding a bike tall enough for your legs to trail, of riding a hill too fast to stop even if you wanted to. At the base of the hill you see the lights turning red.

HOW TO FUCK A MAN YOU
DON'T KNOW

Nine.
It has been a month since you broke up with
Lou. You buy a car so you can drive to and from your
parents' house. They have moved from the fens. The
room that might have been yours is only a tidy spare.
Your mother does not ask you to empty the dishwasher
any more because you are only a guest.

Those late-night, early-morning drives after and
before work are filled with the sound of the shipping
news: that broad, flat voice narrating wind direction
and speed. You are happy to know what will come, what
to prepare for. Sometimes you are so busy listening to
warnings of storms at sea you miss the weather reports
that should really matter to you; get caught in those
flash floods that kill cars and cattle, spend hours sat in
traffic.

When you get there, tired enough to sleep on your feet like a horse, your mother sits you down, tells you that everybody does Internet dating these days, that she understands you are happy alone but you are too nice for it. You never told her about Lou and now, after the event, it is too late to do so. You wish you'd texted her when you first slept with him; told her it was all right, you were having sex and you thought she'd want to know.

Eight.

When you meet someone else you tell yourself it was inevitable, that what you do now is beyond you.

You meet the new one in the pub that you have taken to going to on your own. You enjoy being there, reading and drinking until it gets too busy and you look odd: in your work clothes, a little drunk, red with embarrassment. You see the pregnant girl behind the bar watching you. You wonder if she remembers you meeting Lou there. She must, you think, see people like you all the time.

You used to catch the train, go dancing with your friends. In the city there are clubs where groups of men are not allowed in until women arrive and where the women get in free. You danced in the middle of crowds with your eyes closed, someone else's hands on your hips and back, fingers tangled tight in your hair. Sometimes you'd see their mouths moving; spelling out the digits of phone numbers or wording compliments you pick only stray letters from in the noise.

This is different. His name is Scott. He says he is an actor. He stands at your elbow and starts talking about Iraq and the Booker shortlist. At the time you think this makes him knowing and intellectual. He reads the newspaper, anyway, or listens to Radio 4.

The first time it happens is in the toilet of the pub. When you are done he cleans himself with wet wipes; offers to drive you home though he is drunk enough his eyes focus on spaces beyond your head. He says he is staying in the Travelodge out on the A10; makes a joke about pushing twin beds together. You thank him, give him your number, wait until he is gone and then walk home.

You imagine the drunken crash he is causing on the A-road. It is dark and no one will notice now, but in the morning the road will be strewn with broken bottles of milk, cars burnt to their ribcages, a rotting tractor.

When you go down to the kitchen the next day Lou is listening to the radio in his boxers. You make him tea, toast and scrambled eggs. Arrange to go out for dinner that night to the seafood restaurant you cannot afford but like. Dress nice, put on make-up, carry condoms in your bag. When you feel your phone vibrating between the starter and main you go to the toilet and read the text message from the other one. It feels good in a way you dissect that night, not sleeping. Sort of like masturbating in public or breaking wine glasses.

* * *

Seven.

You are too guilty to say it but it is true. You are bored of Lou, of easy sex; cigarettes, innuendoes, snuggling, spooning, blow jobs, homemade spaghetti bolognese, hangovers, obligatory texting.

You understand now you will have to leave him though you think you are too tired to do it. Again and again you tell yourself you are selfish beyond belief, that if only you left he would find a woman with space enough inside her for a couple of babies, a Land Rover and a golden retriever.

You remind yourself of the night you met, when you held your breath for such a long time he thought you'd drowned. You have been practising in the bath and each time you hold your breath for less time. This in itself seems to mean something awful.

Somehow it has become that you are not the woman for him when all along it was supposed to be the other way around.

Six.

Watch out for the affection. It comes at odd, awful moments, mainly when he is not there: brushing your teeth, opening the door for a parcel, at the photocopying machine. There is nothing much about him you can see which would do this to you. Affection, you tell your housemates, is a sort of sickness. They roll their eyes and tell you they can hear you at night.

That's not affection, you say. That's sex.

You lose conviction in this statement fast. You worry about what is happening to you but it happens anyway. At the cinema you look over the curve of his arm and see other girls looking over other arms back at you. In restaurants he has an uncanny trick of holding your wrist while eating with the other hand. You want to tell him it's very clever but you can't eat that way.

He texts you song lyrics while you're at work and often there are books he has bought you on the bed. You want to tell him you can buy your own books; that you do not want something everybody else is reading, that you are a snob without any taste but that your taste is better than that. You don't.

He sets to trying to make you orgasm as if this is what he was made for. You think his jaw must ache in the mornings; you think his fingers must move involuntarily when he's trying to do other things. You do not tell him the harder he tries the more you feel your orgasm is a conquest, something grey-eyed and eel-shaped with thoughts and digressions all its own.

You see how you irk him. Sometimes you see how you do it on purpose. Catch him wincing at the sound of metal spoons on his Teflon pans; watching his face as you comment on radio shows, television programmes, people on the street. He does not like it when you piss with the door open.

He sees how he irks you and you know he never means to. The way he falls asleep fast as an animal, in the middle of films or on public transport or at night when you can barely sleep two hours through to their end. The way he reads out lines from books, voice cocked up an ironic octave.

You go running and find yourself making long, angry, screaming lists of everything that annoys you about him. The way he eats standing up; the way he forgets people's names; the way he ends texts with his initials.

When you get back you are calm. When you get back you want him again, quick and quiet, his face pillowed into your neck as he finishes. You want him in the mornings, mouth sour on his. You ask him to meet you on your lunch break, find quiet places in cold fields. On the weekends you want nothing more than to stay in bed with him until it gets dark.

There are days you welcome it. Affection is not something which is happening to you; affection is not AIDS or hay fever or a tetanus shot. This is something you have let in of your own volition and it lengthens days into summers. He says you are funny, grasps you round the waist and says you are softening like butter. Listen, you want to tell him. Listen to me.

When he asks you to move in with him you say yes without thinking.

Five.

You try not to let yourself be lulled by the thought of easy sex with someone who's already got past the hurdle of seeing you naked. You understand that easy sex is one of those lies married people tell their single friends.

You have your phone with you at times you shouldn't – half asleep, drinking whilst sad – and text him. You realise you have started something you were not supposed to start. You know only that this is the beginning of the end and that you called it on; you whistled this up. There will be no storm warning; there will be no shipping forecast to pre-empt what will come.

You wait in the Fox and Hound for him. It feels like days have passed. You say his name over and over to make sure you don't forget it: Lou, Lou, Lou. You do not think you will recognise him from the other night but you do. He buys you both a drink. There is no clear moment when you decide it is too late and you like him. Perhaps when he bends his face low over the Guess Who board or when he talks, excited as a child, about the structure of Radiohead songs.

You take him home with you again. When you wake his hands are working already over your hips and chest. You are angry for a moment, as if he were a cat belonging to someone else, snuck in. You want to tell him that he is the one you don't know; he is the one you do not want to know.

Four.

You decide it is the first and only time you will do this and keep all the lights on.

As you take your clothes off, watching him do the same, you think about all the others. If they were older they would always go down on you as soon as you got into the bedroom. They pride themselves on respecting the female orgasm and want you to have one before you fuck. You never did but that's all right.

If they were younger, you wouldn't make it to the bedroom. It's always uncomfortable against the kitchen counter and worse on the carpet, where you get burns on your elbows before you've even done much moving. When they are younger you lose your pants in the hall, their fingers curved like fish hooks, flicking the elastic loose. If they are younger than you they pant with the condom wrapper ripping between their teeth on the pavement outside the front door. You always wanted to tell them they were like dogs at the racetracks, faces rubbed furless in a muzzle and so excited they couldn't even see the rabbit.

It is different from the other times. He knows things they have not known before. He seems to be able to tell when you are bored with a position or when your toes are cramping. He holds your hands above your head at the wrist. You enjoy his tongue in your ear.

After you've done it once he says he wants to sleep. You tell him he can sleep when he's dead, laughing like it's a joke, and, because you feel the urge, take him in your mouth. This is not a promise; this is not a relationship. When he starts to move his hips up and down and holds onto the back of your head you stop.

It is better the second time. His hands on your back, yours round his neck, the edge of the bed shifting you into that position you like; the bolt of his bottom lip between your teeth. He is thinner than you, his hip bones cutting in so you find their marks in the shower the next day.

You are careful not to let the words he says do anything to what you've started. When he says he likes your boobs or that your bottom is tight or that you're pretty fun aren't you, you tell him words are cheap enough to spit and push his face the place you want it to go.

When you find yourself thinking about the slight burr he places on the word legs or the way he pronounces your name a little off-key, you remind yourself he used the word pussy as a pun and move on.

You wake in the night, half asleep, and ask for his number.

Three.

When the others leave, you go to the bar with Gabby and do a shot. You watch the skin on your wrist and arms and her neck as you do it. When you put your shot glass down it makes more noise than it should.

You stand and smoke in the car park. One of the passable ones comes out with his friends and asks to bum a cigarette, asks where's good to go. You pretend you haven't seen him at the fish-and-chip shop or never went to school with his younger brother or didn't catch him, red-faced, in a suit on the way to an interview in the city for a job he wasn't ever going to get.

You watch yourself pretend you've never known anything in your life and never much felt the compulsion to. You want to make him think you have no history or education; that you might have had language once but it's gone now. You want to make him think you're so scrubbed clean of any sort of intelligence that he can lay himself out on you and you'll soak him up.

He says his name is Lou.

You know where you're going. You don't grow up from being young in this town without knowing the only place which is any place is the estuary. You all traipse down there in a row, following the drag lines of smoke. You feed him cigarettes as if they were words. He says he never smokes unless he's drinking. He looks better with one in his mouth, hands free for a couple of breaths.

At the edge of the field you lift one shoe, dark with mud up the thin heel, and tell him he'll have to carry you. You think he has probably pegged you as docile and a little shy – his type – and this is a surprise. His hands holding onto the tops of your thighs feel, for both of you, like an omen.

He carries you all the way and, though you can hear it's pretty hard going near the end, you let him. You let him. At the estuary you slither free without his help and you and Gabby start towards the water. You've done this before.

The water and the white light coming sky-ways. When you were children and it was summer there were no days you did not spend here, stripped to your pants, duck-diving. Your parents told you if you kept going they'd have to keep you in the house; it was dangerous, there were pylons sunk deep into the water there.

More besides, your father would say.

You and your friends would mimic him, a threatening bring-on of a chant: Cars and shopping trolleys and dead foxes and murdered women. Cars and shopping trolleys and dead foxes and murdered women.

You were always better at being in the water than the rest. Sometimes you would come up and they'd be shouting your name, one of them crying.

We thought you drowned. We thought you drowned.

You both take off your tights and shoes but keep the rest of your clothes on. You are not children any more. The men have brought out bottles of cider and are smoking pot. You give him a good look. Take Gabby's hand and jump in. Let go and swim down deep, pylon hunting, reaching out your fingers to find them.

You think: this is how to fuck a man you don't know. This is how to go about forgetting names and syllables.

You used to go out to the estuary at times it was too cold or late for anybody else to be there and practise holding your breath. One day you asked Gabby to come with you. You would not trust anybody else but you trusted her. She sat on the bank with a timer and you went into the water, came out triumphant, sucking in air.

How long? How long?

She was holding the timer tight, her face very still. Fifteen minutes, she said, and you thought maybe you shouldn't have shown her. Fifteen minutes.

This time you do not stay under that long. Imagine him watching from the bank, leant back on his bony elbows talking about amps or video games. You understand the way he thinks. You're his sort of girl, the sort that can't breathe under water any longer than he can.

But you stay under long enough that you feel the star-shaped explosion of his body entering the water. You feel him looking for you, pushing at the water; wait for the hungry gulp of him resurfacing and then follow him up, come up close enough that he can feel you.

Shit, he says. Shit. Gabby is laughing, pulling herself onto the bank as if she'd been an otter before she got bored of it. One of his friends tosses her a beer and in exchange she wrings her hair out onto his lap.

You scull away slowly so he can follow you. Swim out to the middle where the water feels deep enough to drown and feel the ripple of him coming after.

You hold your breath pretty good, he says, as if you were kids playing dares.

You kick up high and then pull the dress over your head. Feel him, solid enough that it must hurt, against your leg. You let him touch your breasts through the thin bra. He gets cold before you.

*   *   *

Two.

You wear that dress. The one that girl Gabby inexplicably likes, called your prostitute dress, pausing to spin her hands through your wardrobe, as if to say: well, one of them anyway. Gabby said she was a relationshipper, a boyfriender. She'd never fuck anybody unless she could see the whites of their children's eyes when he orgasmed.

You put on those red shoes. The others take flats in their bags and they tell you to do the same but you don't.

You go to the Fox and Hound. In a pub in the city you'd be overdressed but here you're fine because there's nowhere else for anybody to go and everybody understands that.

In the pub you all fall into a lexis you know and use without much work. You talk in generalisations, cut bodies down to minor glances, swivel your faces with intent over the rims of your pint or wine glasses. There is a beautiful man in the corner you all think wears his clothes like skin; that isn't the one you want to take home. Men like that know too well what they look like and will make you pay for it later. There are a couple more you use words like not bad and good enough about. You are not bad people; this is just the place you have ended up.

You drink enough to eye round the room with some sort of confidence. Drink enough you feel it in the ends of your fingers, the muscles of your legs. You stop after that. Some of the others are doing shots of tequila or cheap vodka at the bar but you don't join them. You've got a way to go yet.

One.

You do not shave your legs or pubic hair. It is not a wedding night, not a parade or a party or an invitation. You are not a welcome mat.

You speak in aggressions and facts bullet-pointed enough to cut; tell your friends you are going to get laid, this is the night. They laugh and open wine or sprawl out on their elbows and look at you. Say: yeah. Do it. They've heard it from you before and from themselves and mostly it's just something that tastes pretty good in your mouth. This is different. You don't need to tell them that.

They will know what has happened later: from the sound of the bed against the wall or the funnel noise of piss falling into the toilet from a standing height or from meeting him in the morning, trapped trying to open the front door.

LANGUAGE

HARROW WILLIAMS was the sort of boy who got away with things. Harrow Williams was not fat, only big; built through with power. She was not small-boned herself, you could have that fact for nothing, but what she liked most about Harrow was that he was taller than all the other boys and spanned across the shoulders like a bear. He'd been big when he was a child, violent with it, but had only seemed now to grow into his size. She'd loved him since they were four and he'd leant over, planted a red-paint handprint onto her chest, almost knocking her down. As if he owned her already.

And what sort of a device was she? At sixteen Nora Marlow Carr was good at all those things nobody much wanted to be good at. She could do maths in her head the way other people came up with sentences; remembered pretty much everything she saw written down or heard told to her; knew the ins and outs of string theory and could, if she had the urge, take apart a hefty radio and jam it back together. She didn't sleep much and she knew it made her look like someone had beaten her about the face, but there it was. She was larger than was fashionable; sometimes caught herself looking with something akin to lust at all those bones that protruded out of girls at school; the solipsism of legs and arms, the buds of them. Mostly, though, she thought they looked as if they hadn't grown properly. She understood – because she was logical and somewhat cold with it – that they saw her with the same confusion; imagined her bready with everything she carried, watched with distaste the motion of her childbearing hips, her milk-carrying breasts and wave-making thighs. She was a natural woman, they sang to one another under their breath when they saw her, and meant nothing good by it.

Harrow had worked through those bony women and them through him and she'd watched with dry fascination. In reception, it was little Marty Brewer who was the first girl to have her ears pierced and who held his hand for a day before holding someone else's. Nora listened to the gossip, knew Harrow liked to take a girl on the bus to the cinema in the city and then to Subway. If he liked you enough he'd kiss you on the way back. Later she knew, because she understood about biology, there was more than hand-holding going on.

The year she turned sixteen she decided enough was enough. She was not the sort of girl who waited for something to come her way and, if she wanted a thing bad enough, she thought she could probably find a way to get it. She waited until after sports when all the other boys had gone home and Harrow was out with Ms Hasin practising for the 2,000 metres. He was heavy for a track runner but there was enough power in those limbs – legs more like a horse than a boy. Everybody said he was building himself up for the next Olympics.

She went out into the car park and leant against his car and when he came walking up she looked at him. There was no one else there.

He screwed up his face so lines appeared between his nose and around his eyes.

Nora, right? he said, as if they hadn't been in the same school since they were four, as if he'd never planted that red handprint. Well, that didn't matter now.

She thought the most beautiful thing she'd ever heard was entanglement theory. She told Harrow that was what they were: two particles forever linked and fated to change one another. He looked at her askance and she tried hard to think how to put it into a language he would understand.

When she looked back at him he'd taken his cock out. It was not miraculous the way she'd imagined, not beautiful or serene or possessed of any great power. All the same she liked the strange nod of it moving seemingly unconnected to the rest, recognised it was circumcised and liked that; liked the small, dark spots at its base.

You need me to tell you what to do? Harrow said.

She shook her head. She'd read the literature.

Harrow meant it to be a one-time event and that was a fine thing for him to think, but she knew he didn't really understand entanglement theory at all, only liked hearing things he couldn't comprehend, and that it would be a while longer before they'd shake one another.

She knew the way it worked. She was supposed to be coy and shy and give him her home number and wait to see if he'd call her.

That was one way of going about it.

She rang him the next night until he picked up. Didn't let him speak but told him everything she was going to do to him. When she was done she stopped and let him think on it.

All right, he said.

His mother worked the night shift and her parents hadn't ever worried she was the sneaking-out type, so they met at his. She knew why it was so good, why it was better than everything she'd overheard from the girls at school who spoke about it with a sort of aged disappointment. Because he didn't think he had to treat her the way he would one of the skinny women he'd marry, and she had nothing to lose. Afterwards he gave her the lines he'd picked up from American films and she let him get them out: he wasn't looking for a relationship, he just wanted to have some fun; she was a great girl, she really was.

I'm coming over, she would tell him at school or she'd text him when she was already out the window, sliding down the roof slope, dropping to the grass. Sometimes he said: well, I told you I'm not looking for anything of the frequent-flyer persuasion, or he'd shake his head and say he wished he could, he really did, but his evening had pretty big plans wound up in it. That line only held fast the time it took for her to get her bra off.

When he said it, she knew it surprised him more than her. She let it rest between them for a moment with his face sort of stiffening as if he'd been electrocuted. Then she said: well, yes. Me too. And that was that. Harrow Williams was the sort of boy who only held one state of mind at a time and once he decided they were on, there was nothing he or anybody else could do about it. She told him she didn't believe in marriage, that nothing she was ever going to do was for the government or god or anything else beginning with g and that marriage was just a force of control. He looked at her the way he did when she said things he didn't understand; but after they'd had sex, he told her if she wanted to live at his house they'd need to get it done.

She'd never really given up something for anyone. You could do anything else, she told herself; you could break everything in half and scoop out the middle and put it back in. You could write a book or a play or cure infertility. She was eighteen and school was done and she could go to Cambridge or Oxford or London and study maths or English. She could travel. Except she had time for all that. And she had time for him.

If you don't want to marry me you don't have to, he said, a little sulky with it.

I do want to. OK?

Yeah. OK.

Her parents didn't like to argue but, after she told them, she caught them studying her face in a sort of confusion. As if they would discover, looking hard enough, the trick of the matter, the deal she'd been forced into. As if she would slide a note across to them if they waited long enough and it would say: *Help me.*

At the wedding she turned and looked at their bemused faces. There was no one there but them and Harrow's mother, who was dressed in red and crying. Nora waited for the day to be over and then it was.

She wished someone had told her what living with a man was like. She would not have changed tack but she thought, all the same, a degree of warning would have been good. The musky smell; the stains on the toilet he did not seem to see; the handfuls of tissue she pulled out from down the side of the bed. There were days she thought on what she'd given away. Days she tried to read two books at a time to catch up. Days she went into the city and handed out CVs and saw what little she could get with good marks at school and an attractive husband.

Even then there was never a consideration of going. The shape of him beneath her hands in the morning, the words he said when he was sleepy enough not to think about them, the way he remembered things she told him.

Well, except Harrow had died. Barely a year and she only nineteen, but there it was. She stood next to his mother at the hospital and thought she understood what they were saying except she was certain they were wrong. There wasn't a blood clot in his lung that had, probably, been there since he was born and only now exploded. That was not what had happened. Harrow, she was certain, had died because he decided he loved her after all. He was an eight or a nine and she was a three or a four and the maths of that all added up to Harrow never having been hers to begin with.

At the funeral her parents told her she had to come home, had to grow a life out of whatever she had. They talked about universities and scholarships and jobs in the city and fish in the sea. They were the way she used to be, she saw that now: they were doers. She told them she would get around to it but right now she had to look after Harrow's mother and she hoped they understood.

She was called Sarah and was older than most of the other parents. Nora thought her sort of beautiful; she looked, anyway, a bit like Harrow and held herself in the same unselfconscious way. She'd not seemed to have much comment to make on them marrying but she had, Nora thought, liked her.

Those days Sarah didn't always seem to know where she was and sometimes she talked about Harrow as if he'd just gone out for a stroll or was running errands. Though these were not things Harrow would ever have done.

Nora did the cooking and cleaned and the rest of the time she read or sat in the sort of stupor that comes from losing the trick of sleeping. She didn't try any more. There wasn't any use trying once it had gone that way.

Nora knew what people said about her. She was up-and-down odd and now Harrow was gone she should move on into a life that more befitted a broad-hipped, glasses-wearing girl who looked – well, it was fine – old before her time.

Part of her always thought Harrow would come back. Maybe she thought it because they were particles entangled. Or because her want was surely strong enough to curse him awake. Or because she'd given up things and – a balancing – needed something in return.

In the end it was none of these things. It was only Sarah.

What are you doing? Nora asked when she found the fragments of tiny animal bones in the bin, tripped over piles of smooth stones in the front garden, tried to make sense of the small dirt offerings: in a cup in the airing cupboard, under her bed, in the bath.

Sarah would not answer her, went out into the garden with her mixing bowl.

When Harrow came back Nora decided she wasn't going to overthink it. Only be a little grateful she hadn't argued harder for a cremation the way she'd wanted to.

There was dirt all over him and he must have – the way they did in the films – dug himself out because there was blood on his hands and most of his nails were cut badly.

Sarah had brought him back, wished him out. Still – she put the kitchen table between her and him and, scouting around for something to wield, picked up the rolling pin and held it at chest height.

It's all right, Nora said. She held her hand up to Harrow's mouth. He pressed his lips to it hard, leaving a dirt-shaped kiss, and she saw that he was just as relieved as she was.

Let's run a bath, she said. He'll be fine when he's clean.

She took off his suit in the bathroom and then poked and prodded till he climbed into the hot water and stood, arms swinging a little. He wouldn't sit down so she got the sponge and scrubbed until he looked as clean as she could manage, then she towelled him down. He didn't

80

say anything, though he followed her motions with his eyes, touched her hands. She didn't say anything either, only waited. Outside the bathroom she could hear Sarah waiting too.

There were signs she could have read off him that she did not see or chose to ignore: his breathing high and a little laboured, as if air didn't work well in him any more; the odd smell of him: like concrete setting or the cold dredged up on riverbanks.

In the morning she turned in the bed and he was looking at her the way he used to across the classroom or as they passed in the hall when everything they were doing was a secret so he could save face. She felt the rise of him against her leg, held him in her fist and moved her hand. A little later, feeling the comfortable known of his hips against hers, she thought that his time away had lost them nothing, had given them only a perspective of loss. A knowledge of absence. Except, when he arched back his head, mouth open, and let out a one-syllabled word, there was a sharp pain in the roof of her mouth. She rolled out from under him. He lay back, one hand under his head, sweat on his forehead and neck.

Are you all right?

She put a hand over her lips, eyes watering, probed the roof of her mouth with her tongue, felt the pulse of ulcers gathering in rings.

What is it?

It was clear now: again the skid of hurt against her teeth at his words. She rocked back off the bed, one hand warding him away, though he followed, dog-like, reaching out. She caught the door in her fist, shut it between them. His voice, coming muffled through the wood, burnt her mouth and eyes.

What is it? Sarah said, coming down the hallway.

Nora watched, clenching her teeth, as the force of Harrow's muffled words started to hit Sarah's face.

The impact of Harrow's language on Sarah seemed much worse than it was on her – a single syllable eliciting vomiting, sentences starting nosebleeds – so Nora took Harrow to the garage and sat with the door pulled closed.

He wrote: *I don't want to.*

She told him she didn't care. Turned the light out so he couldn't see what was happening to her. Gripped him by the wrist and told him what to do.

They tried out all the letters one by one, cycling through the alphabet twice until she dug her nails hard into his palms and then he was quiet. They worked through nouns, verbs, adjectives. She made him try out adverbs, pronouns and prepositions. She tested herself by waiting for pain, noting down the area and velocity at which it came. When a word seemed to elicit less pain or appear in an area which seemed less extreme (for example her arms or legs as opposed to her face or torso) she squeezed his hand twice to make him repeat it. Mostly the word repeated would bring on pain in a different area or of a different type and then they would carry on. If the word caused in any way a similar reaction she noted it down.

At first the word 'partial' seemed to have a reaction less extreme than others. This was later proved to be otherwise. At first the phrase 'wanted scrabble she' appeared to elicit pain after a longer than normal waiting period. This too turned out to be incorrect.

But if anyone could fix him it was her.

She caught the neighbour's rabbit on one of its escape trips and brought it down in her arms into the garage.

He wrote: *That's enough. I don't need to speak.*

She held the rabbit, not wriggling, only sniffing a little, in her arms. Come on, she said.

He wrote: *Fuck you backwards with a broomstick.*

She told him to go through his consonants the way they'd done before and she would tell him when to stop. She sat numbly as he did it, holding the rabbit. It fought her. She could feel his words on its body.

Later she went round with the rabbit in a plastic bag, told them she'd found it in the garden.

At the end of the week they caught him trying to jemmy the window with a slat broken off his bed. Sarah went down quickly under the onslaught he unleashed against them – unconnected words, curses, quotes Nora recognised from films, the names of people they'd gone to school with. He only stopped when Nora caught, with her finger, the quick trickle of blood from her own nostril, raised her hand to show him.

Most days, when she woke, she could feel it was too late anyway; his words were in her system like a sickness. She could feel the spiky pressure of letters against her gut, the sticks of Ks and Ts and Ls on her insides. She could hear Sarah coughing as if something, a spark plug or wire, had come loose in her. They were not sleeping in the same bed because – though he never had before – he'd started talking in his sleep.

One morning she made a cup of tea, went and opened the door to the sitting room. He was asleep on the sofa. She tightened her stomach in case of an involuntary syllable, a slipped-out sentence. Asleep he looked as if he were an animal, something quiet and wondering, something beautifully thoughtless. She bent to wake him the way she always used to, a slipped tongue in his ear, but, at his eyes flickering, she panicked, dropped the cup of tea, clapped a hand across his mouth to silence whatever might be coming.

She saw the look in his eyes: reproachful, angry. Tried to kiss it away, wiping the hot tea off him with her hands and mouth, felt only that look trained on her while she did.

The house was now perpetually twilight; all the curtains drawn so nobody would see what had come back to them. She and Harrow spent days on the sofa, pen and paper between them, writing long notes to one another, legs tangled beneath the blanket. Once he wrote: *Tell me about the particles.* Slipped a hand beneath the edge of her dressing gown. Wrote: *How does this feel? What does this feel like?*

She could hear – pretended not to and watched him doing the same – Sarah hacking something up in the bathroom.

Most days were not like that. *I'm trapped.* He wrote: *I'm going fucking mad.* She ordered him television box sets; ordered him a running machine which he stood and watched her putting together and then refused to use; ordered him books and exotic food and audio tapes.

Let me go out, he wrote, sat across the kitchen table from her. *I'll wear a hood. Just for an hour. Just for a moment. Nobody will notice.* She shook her head.

She sat and watched him wolfing, restless, about the sitting room. The floor was covered in the spread of half-finished jigsaws, half-played games of Monopoly and Cluedo. Now and then a television programme would be turned on but it only ever lasted a moment before the channel was changed. She watched him doing press-ups on the sitting-room floor or pulling himself up by the lintel of a door and, though she had seen this before, he seemed to do it with a new ease, barely breaking a sweat.

It took another month for the words he wrote to become infected too. Sarah was making a concerted effort to spend time with him, though more and more she looked as if she were emptying out of her body, thinning away to nothing. Nora would leave them alone in the kitchen, listen to the strange tick-over of their conversation: the scratch of Harrow's pen on the paper, the slow answers Sarah gave. (Harrow asked things on the page he would never have asked, or thought to ask, when he was verbal.) She listened to the pauses between his questions and Sarah's answers. At one point she could hear him writing for a long time, the fast sound of the words. She could hear it still as she made three cups of tea, carried them in on a tray. There were red blisters coming up on Sarah's arms, on her chest and face. Harrow had not noticed, was writing and writing with a sort of furious intent, nose almost touching the page. Nora tore it away from him and, for a second, he wrote on the table, the letters etched in.

She put Sarah to bed and then went round the house finding all the scattered pages of his words and pushed them into the bin bag. She tried not to see them, those dense, tight little letters against the sick white of the paper; but by the time she was done, she'd caught sight of enough half-words that she had to rest against the corridor wall, breathing hard.

She took the pages out into the garden. Crossed the back field and balled them up and set fire to them. She stood there till it was done. Stood and wondered if the ash would destroy the crop when it grew. The cold air burnt the rash the pages had raised on her arms and chest.

It doesn't matter, she told him when she went back in. He was still sat at the kitchen table. She picked up the pen and put it in the bin, watched his eyes following her. It doesn't matter. She pressed her nose against the solid bone of his face.

Doesn't it?

She bent double. Straightened with difficulty to look at him. He looked back as if she were a creature he'd never seen before.

They spent the rest of the day at the table devising a system of signs. They came up with hand motions for all the words he cared most about. When they were done he seemed changed, smiling at her. He pointed at himself with one finger, jabbed the finger into the O of his other fist, then pointed at her.

She took off her clothes, laughed as he jerked his hands around, forming signs they hadn't discovered yet, commenting. The impact of his language on her over the weeks was clear. She'd never been bony before but she almost was now, the press of ribs more bruise than anything else, the stretch of cheekbone. She took his clothes off, looked for a change on him. He was not loosening the way she'd thought he might. Instead he seemed bigger, stronger; the muscles defined on his chest. She was – no time to stop the feeling – afraid of him.

The mass of him: his hands were the size of books flattened open.

He could have stopped her; he could have done anything he wanted. He only watched with wide, brown eyes; let her ball a sock into his mouth, fasten his wrists to the chair with the handcuffs he'd bought her. She pressed her knees into either side of his body as if she could burrow on in if she tried hard enough. She wanted this to mean: nothing has changed. She wanted this to mean: there are signs for everything we can think of and it's not a language anyone else needs to know.

When she was done she pulled the sock out so she could press her mouth to his. Sat straight to look down at him and, when he smiled, felt the wordless expression rot into her insides, sharp explosions of pain in her mouth and on her hands and face and chest.

She kicked backwards, pressed her knuckles eye-ways so she could not see him. On the floor she fell over the scattered remains of his livings: half-full teacups, board games he'd been playing against himself.

I don't want, he said –

Beneath her foot a plate was broken.

– to hurt you. Each word was an attack and before each word she could feel the thought of it – like an echo preceding its sound.

In the corridor on the way to their room his words brought her down and she went on hands and knees. At the bedroom she pushed the door closed, put her weight against it and put her hands over her ears. She could hear the churn of his brain, the guttering end of half-formed thoughts. Most of them were roars that deafened everything else out of her.

She stuffed the gap at the bottom of the door with T-shirts, played music loud. It did not matter. It did not matter that she could not hear if he spoke, that she'd burnt every fragment of his writing: his thoughts were loud enough to blister, to inch belly-ways and shard outwards.

She'd explained to herself before and – though the words didn't taste as good and fresh as they had that first time – did it again now: you could do anything. There was a coil of rope in the wardrobe. The handcuffs were still in the sitting room; she would have to do without. At the last moment, the click of his thoughts turning in her, she snapped two rungs off a chair, held them together: a wobbly cross. She would cover her bases. There were lines from the Qur'an she'd learnt once; stray phrases from the Torah and the Old Testament that she mouthed over, tried to hold onto.

She closed her eyes and took the hallway blind, not touching the walls. There was the smell – though she had not noticed it before – of something turning bad. She could feel the dull pulse of his living, a sucking heat. Expected, every moment, to come upon a mass of muscle, a mouth poised open. In the bathroom she emptied the cabinet of sleeping pills.

She could hear words from somewhere in the house, loud enough to be spoken though she knew they were not: a jumbled flow of thought syllables. There was blood in the sink when she coughed and a wrench in her arms when she moved.

She knew the plan well. And though there were someone else's thoughts hooked and barbed inside her, she saw the dark passage of where she was going: not a rescue at all, only a stripping away, a cursing back into nothing.

THE SUPERSTITION OF
ALBATROSS

POLLY,

I've been thinking about you and the baby. I think the baby is probably thinking about me too. You remember that story where storks bring little ones in packages? You watching out?

We're out far now. You think you know what that means but it doesn't mean anything till you're here. We couldn't go back if we wanted to.

There had been four, count them, four letters from him before there was nothing. Nobody said it but she knew what they were thinking: he'd made his getaway while he still could. Her feet were so swollen all she could fit into were wellingtons. Never mind. She put on a coat and the cat came stalking after her and onto the bus before she could stop it. Squalled up and down the aisle, pissed at her feet. She held it tight on the changes, fumbled for exact money. Three buses and a train and finally a dock hardly anyone had heard of.

You seen him then? she said to the men on the boats tied up there. They eyed her belly and she wondered if there was a superstition about a pregnant woman on her own or about a pregnant woman who didn't love what she carried half as much as she should, or simply a superstition about a woman, filled up or not.

Well? she said, rapping a fist on the gunwale three times: her own sort of curse for them.

They shook their heads. She'd heard stories about post ships robbed for their cargo, pirates lonely enough to take anything that smelt of someone else's home, even if they didn't understand the lingo. She dreamt of that: a man with hair white before its time, hunched low over a letter whose words he could not read.

On the way back to town she got lost, slept at a bus station with the cat tied to her wrist with string. In the morning nobody knew where she was going though she wrote the name of the town down when they asked. She would not leave again.

She'd known him all through school but it wasn't till they were both seventeen and in the Fox and Hound that she pulled up to the bar next to him, elbow to elbow, raised an eyebrow. There wasn't any use pretending.

He was superstitious as an old fish wife. In the beer garden behind the pub she asked if he had a condom.

I can't use those, he said stiffly, as if she'd asked something inappropriate. They're like broken mirrors.

What? Polly said, pulling back.

Broken mirrors, he said. Except more bad luck. Longer than seven years anyway.

If she hadn't been drinking up the courage to talk to him all night and then after that drinking to keep the nerve and after that drinking as something to do, she wouldn't have let him.

When she told him what he'd done, a month later and she vomiting enough to know, he towed her along the street and straight into the chapel.

What we doing here? What the fuck are we doing here?

Shut up.

He fell to his knees with a purpose she'd seen in him only twice, once in the dank pub garden, fumblingly, and once, barely fifteen, as he skidded towards her, mouth open, arms wide to tackle her down.

What you going to do? she said later.

He turned his head in a pained sort of way. She said his name till he looked at her. How you going to make money, Ruben? He looked like a child who'd got himself lost somewhere. They were sat on the grey cemetery wall and she let him think on it, getting more and more impatient. There was a tractor turning across the field in front of them. Cutting through the corn. She watched him narrowly as he stared at it.

I got a thought, he said.

Is that right?

He looked at her proper then, tapping his nose with the broad of his thumb. She looked at the rash of freckles across his face, clicked her tongue at him until he laughed. The next day he was gone and it took asking more than one person to work out where he was, and even then nobody knew the name of the place or how he'd get back from there.

He loved the parts of the boat, the bits that made it up, that brought it together; loved the tangy names for things; loved the rules of it. He loved, most of all, the secret codes of fear and belief the boats ran on. Came home every other week with his fingers nicked like a crabber and leant across the little table she'd got from her mother and told her only the captain was allowed to whistle at sea in case you whistled up the wrong sort of wind; how you had to step on board with your right foot each time and that they called old Kerri Finney a Jonah down the docks because of the bad luck he brought to journeys. He talked often about an old, burnt-out lighthouse and the stories the others told about it.

You have to call a hare a langlugs, he'd said. And you can't ever let them on the boat. Not ever.

She wanted to stand up, turn sideways, point to the mooning thing that hung out in front of her and say: and what exactly do you think about this?

I'd let a hare on board, she'd say instead.

S'not a hare, he said, frog-eyed above his sharp cheeks. It's a langlugs. I told you. I told you.

All right.

At first it was all fishing boats, trawlers and low riders with nets. Except he didn't want to do that, didn't want to wake up dark early and spend all day raw-handed, pulling in catches, smelling of fish forever. He wanted, he said, to be on one of the boats that sailed out far enough there wasn't coast for two weeks, nothing but sea and brine, wanted to work on one of the ships sailed to the Caribbean for rich owners or ploughed to the tip of Africa.

Well, she said – and thought, without saying it out loud, he'd never find one to take him, skinny as he was and where he was from and who his parents were. Boats like that probably cared about things like blood.

The last day before he left for good, he came in late, coat front bulging, something moving beneath it, rolling out onto the kitchen table and up into an angry triangle shape. Not black but greying right up to the spatters of white that pillowed its face, turning on the table to observe her with mute rage.

What the bloody hell is that?

It's a cat.

She felt, then, how all his old mythic beliefs had somehow burrowed into her, just like his baby had.

Bad luck, that's what you said.

He reached out a hand, grinning his freckles narrow. The cat took a swipe at him.

It's good luck for sailors. Interesting, isn't it? And for sailors' wives. You'll keep me safe by having her here. The cat burrowed backwards on its haunches, took another rising step towards his face.

That night he told her about the albatross; birds who carried the souls of dead sailors and what did she think about that? She said she didn't think anything about it and he stuck his tongue out against her face until she laughed. Later she opened her eyes and saw him looking at her, his pupils very wide, his breathing a little uneven.

What?

That sounds all right, doesn't it?

What? What sounds all right?

Being in an albatross. Flying around and everything.

What are you talking about?

It sounds good.

All right. Quiet now.

He nudged closer like he was trying to flip back the braces of her skin and climb on in. Like there was comfort in there as much as in the thought of dying only to wake as a passenger in an albatross's body.

What about you and the baby, though. Where will you go?

She laughed. I don't know. I could be happy inside a pigeon.

His face didn't change any. She closed her eyes to cut it out.

He wrote to her about being on watch at three in the morning and seeing the cutting lights of another ship coming across the fog water. On the radio to them, watching them steaming on closer. On the radio to nothing but silence. Sometimes when he wrote they were ghost ships, abandoned and left to keen their own way. Sometimes they were only Greeks with not enough crew or patience to man the night shifts.

She got a job to fill the hours before sleeping, worked in the Fox and Hound, watched her belly swelling like it was air blown. Wished it air blown. Wished it always. Dreamt at night of the ships turned loose across the water, dreamt she swam to one and wound her way up the rope and left a wet footprint trail through the empty rooms, the half-eaten plates of food, barely cold beds, the spattering sound of the fish in the hold coming back to life.

He wrote to her about the line-crossing ceremony they enacted at the equator, like a prayer, and about the photo of the pig the captain kept as good luck, and the plant somebody put on board to curse them and which he kicked with a boot so it swung high, turned over itself and then dropped down into the water.

She did not name the cat out of defiance but after a week they set up a begrudging house fellowship. The skinny body barely enough to keep itself warm though it tried to help, perched atop her belly, not purring, rather shaking a little, as if it had never been taught how. In exchange, twice a week she bought it a fish, watched it pick around the bones, fed it tinned sardines the rest of the time, woke in the morning to its curious face examining her.

In the photo he sent he was bare-chested, tanned as a nut, arm turned to show off the wobbly inked lines: a north star. *So I can find my way back*, he wrote. What would she have written if there was a place to send it? Don't come back. I don't want you.

Remember about the albatrosses? We got one on our tail now. I didn't know what it was when I saw it. It was too big to be anything real. I keep thinking about them carrying dead sailors around inside them. How creepy is that? Like someone's looking out his big eyes at us. The others are throwing up bits of bread and the rest to him but he won't swoop to get them the way seagulls will. He's got pride. He waits till they've fallen and then goes without even much moving his wings. I don't throw bread to him and sometimes I think he's eyeing me because of it. He knows that he worries me a bit. The others are taking the piss and they are right. I've got too much fear in me.

Silence now. Never mind. Never mind him. She picked up more work, worked the late shift because it paid better and because she liked emptying out the pub, turfing out the old ones who came every night and still bowed their heads thoughtfully at the sight of her stomach. Walking home the sky gave everything away and when it was pink she felt a toggle of fear, tried not to but couldn't help remembering Ruben coming jogging back along the path because the sky was red and did she feel all right?

Strange how things she thought she'd never really listened to had got in anyway. She took daily note of what fell on the floor, of what was on the table when she went down, of the first person who came into the pub in the afternoon. She took fearful notice of the rabbits strung in the butcher's window and, one night, when she wasn't working and didn't know what to do, she carved a compass onto the kitchen table, as wobbly and ugly as Ruben's tattoo.

Some days it felt like a boat, that house, wet in all the corners and running in seams up to the ceiling, all the furniture bolted to the walls. Some days she felt there were waves, rip tides and countercurrents, tripping beneath the floorboards, rolling behind her when she wasn't looking, upsetting the uneasy balance. Some days she felt there were sea creatures dredged up in there too, come back instead of him: shoals jittering over her legs at night, great breathing somethings disturbing the carpet line, shellfish washed up in the bath.

Soon the sky was red most mornings and the cat came down with something, sneezing often, throwing up anything she gave it. The sky was red most mornings and when she came downstairs it was like a storm had been taken out of a jar and let go in the house, everything from the table and the counters and the walls on the floor.

When she wasn't working she read over his four letters. Angrier and angrier: for giving him anything let alone her time. Read them like there were clues shoved up behind the words or inking out from the full stops: a part of the message she had missed, where he told her he wouldn't be coming back, that he wanted a baby about as much as she did and he was going to stay away. Except she knew really she wouldn't find anything. He didn't write the sort of words that could hide anything anywhere.

At night she couldn't sleep for the whales that came breaching up through the house's watery foundations, rent apart the floorboards to flip through, circled the bed in sharkish lines until that is what they were: sharks made from all the letters he'd used to describe them, right up to the tottering S that made up the apex of each fin.

It was harder being left behind. Because sometimes the sharks grew legs, moaning from the pain: white, thin limbs with bony ankles. They climbed onto the bed and lay down next to her until there were so many there wasn't room and then they piled on top. They wanted to tell her how hard it was to have what they had: grey, waterproof bodies you had to keep moving otherwise you'd die, and legs like supermodels. They were always off balance and she pitied them until she couldn't breathe.

She started going to the pub even when she wasn't working. Took the four letters and read them leaning on the counter with the chair pushed back to accommodate the jut of her. Once she looked around and saw herself for what she'd become: a local like the rest of them, all balled up inside themselves, all in their usual seats.

At the weekends and on Friday nights the pub was full up, full right up. There were bodies on either side of her and foam on the countertop and sometimes she went round and helped even if she wasn't getting paid for her time.

Once she turned to the sight of an arm bearing the inked shape of a compass, felt a wrench and looked up. They didn't get sailors there often. They didn't often get anybody who hadn't been born there. It was far enough from anything and everything. He was older than Ruben, looking wryly up at her like he knew she'd seen the dash of someone else reflected on him. She stayed close by him through the night, saw the ends and starts of conversations swimming up and then receding into the loud. Boat words she knew from Ruben caught at her like hooks.

You been long? he said later, lowering his chin at her stomach. The pub was emptying out.

Eight months. Maybe a bit more.

He drew air into his cheeks but did not let the whistle out. He had an accent she did not know. Not a fen one anyway. Maybe not an English one.

Getting there. Aren't you.

She did not answer. When she came back he was gone, drink only half finished.

She wiped the beer slicks and laid the letter flat, bending her head to read it.

The thing is, what with thinking on you and the baby, and seeing him following us, I can't shake the thought that it's not storks at all. It's him. He knows I've got one on the way and he's thinking on whether to bring him or not. He's testing me. We lost him in the fog. I think he got bored and went off. I keep having these nightmares, though. They bring the babies and then take them away again. It's bad luck to say so but I'm glad the bird is gone. Is the cat OK?

One morning she woke and the sky was red enough it came glazed through the curtains. She felt sick through to her bones. A great, seasick nausea. Off kilter. Went down the steps one at a time, one hand on the wall. Something had happened. Sometimes it was easy to know. The hot sunrise was at her temples and filling her mouth.

The albatross was on top of the kitchen table, one foot on either side of the carved compass. Behind it the window was broken through, pushed in with the frame bent down. The great span of its wings was open, measuring space. The light picked it out through the broken window and it looked like a mistake nobody was ever meant to see. She remembered the words Ruben had used when he wrote about them: the hazed shapes cutting through without moving, the coming of them as if called. It was stone heavy, head hanging down, wings straining at the chest. She could see the breath shifting, the stir of it.

She stepped down and onto something broken, hissed, felt the skin open. The bird on her table shook itself up, returned its wings against its ribcage, balanced up on its huge, flattened feet.

She wanted to say to it: I know why you're here; I know why you've come. I wished it away, I know I did. I wished you here.

She imagined, one hand going to her belly, Ruben, wherever he was – under the sea or islanded up somewhere or just out sailing and tanning and peeling oranges with his clever fingers. She saw him sitting up and knowing, though he'd never known anything in his life, what she'd called up. Well, he would be praying. That was what he did.

I've got too many thoughts – you never said it but I'm sure you were thinking it! Never mind. I'm getting sensible for you. I'm working up a build and I'll come home to you and the baby.

She took another step forward and the bird gave her eye contact as if that was all it needed for everything to be as it should be. That was a sort of prayer in itself, she thought, bringing a hand up.

A HEAVY DEVOTION

THERE IS nothing much to eat but there is tea if you would like some.

Near the beginning people came all the time. There was a journalist who sat where you are sitting now. It was winter. He said his car had broken down outside town though we both knew that was a lie. I thought you looked a little like him out the window but I see now I was wrong. Are you one of the followers? They come sometimes too.

There are times I hear about my son. You have to know what you are looking for and I've been looking long enough to know. Someone in the North drawing crowds, saying they can hold their breath for hours; someone along the coast hunting hospitals, breaking into rooms.

Do you want to see the photos of him? There are some from when he was older; ones he sent to me. Do you want to see the room he slept in? People normally want to see that. No? I can tell you about him anyway. It's been a while since anyone visited.

He came big; came with a slick of dark hair almost to his shoulders and a set of fine white teeth that bit onto my finger. It was the summer the fields flooded and stayed that way so long all the trees rotted to pulp. I took him to meet my friends and they all held him and bounced him on their knees. He was a quiet baby. He made little fuss. We passed him round the table in the pub. I almost forgot, then – watching him move from hand to hand – what he was.

The first time it happened he was still small. A little twisted shape of skin and bone, narrow wrists balancing big, heavy hands. He was useless, wrenching from side to side on his back, legs pedalling like a beetle. I was not afraid of him then. He was sickly, caught colds, had a cough all the time. I kept the house warm and we stayed mostly here, in the kitchen. I filled the sink with warm water, held him. He liked it there.

To begin with I didn't understand. There was an ache. Here. Across my belly. I don't remember what the first thing to go was. Only that it was a single word, a city I'd been thinking of perhaps, or my mother's maiden name. He made a sound. A gurgle, I thought. Though it was a word. He was excited by it, thrashing in my hands. I tried to say the word back to him but there was nothing there. An absence.

That first week I lost things fast. Single words, whole memories, sentences I'd once said to someone. He took what I said or was thinking. At the start I wrote lists of all the words I wanted to keep, tested myself on questions when he was asleep. *What is the name of the town you live in? How old are you?* Those are the ones he took first. The ones I needed most.

I left him in the bedroom with the sides of the cot locked. It did not make any difference what room he was in. Doors and walls and locks had no power.

I thought of treating him the way they would hundreds of years ago. Leaving him out where the cold or the foxes would get him. But that was not a thing possible to do.

He grew fast with his takings. Faster than I could have imagined. His hair was longer than mine. I plaited it, tied it in a tight knot on top of his head. When he slept he tore it loose and lay beneath it. His toenails were claws. I cut them warily, watching his face while he watched me do it. He looked like me. More and more. The colour of his eyes, the shape of his face, his shoulders.

He was barely a year old though after the first few stealings he'd crawled and soon after that I caught him walking, stumbling from one piece of furniture to the next, clinging on. Turning his big smile towards me.

Do you remember – he would say after that. I would shake my head. He talked about days I was certain had

107

been mine, people I thought I must have known. In the shop he would run ahead, stalking around the aisles. Look, he would say, pointing at someone I did not remember. Look. And people would stare.

Do you want something to eat or drink? You don't look comfortable. It is cold, I know. I have not been to the shop but there might be tea or something in the cupboards. You're free to look. You can stay until it gets dark. You don't talk much.

Some people came to the house once. They wore stiff green coats and woollen hats though it was a hot summer. I knew I made them nervous because I looked like him; I walked and talked the way he did. I did not want to let them in but beneath their coats they were bunched with muscle, thick at the neck and shoulder. Their bodies were heavy devotion. They wanted only caffeine-free – I did not have it – they would not drink the beer I gave them.

They sat on the edge of the sofa, tipped forwards onto the shined toes of their shoes. When I moved my hands or face I could see them wince; I looked like a mistake who'd stolen his shape. I wanted to tell them that was not the way it was.

What can you tell us about him?

I got out the photos I keep in the drawer. He did not like them to be taken, most were of the back of his head or the flat of his hand raised in protest. There were scabs on his knees, his nose broken from when he fell off his bike. They were not interested in that; did not want to see him that way.

Tell us about the things he did, they said and I knew what they wanted me to say. One got out a notebook and balanced it on the huge bridge of his knee, held the pen in his fist.

What did he do to the heating?

They tilted further forward.

He didn't do anything to the heating.

What about when you had meat, one said. He stood, legs splayed.

Nothing happened when we had meat, I said.

Maybe, the one with the notebook said, you didn't notice when the meat was better than you first thought, more free range.

An easy mistake, said the other.

I would give them nothing. They got desperate. They asked if he ever saved roadkill.

Maybe he fixed your washing machine or television when it broke.

They didn't break, I said.

People came over the years, though they quickly learnt I was no good for it. Some mornings there were threats: soft, stinking packages pushed through the letter box, broken windows. They wrote things on the Internet I will not repeat. They came less and less. I was no good as a mythmaker. Never have been.

*　*　*

Yes, you can come closer if you want. Sit here, by the lamp. Are you someone who knew him? Maybe you could tell me about him. I would like to hear about the way he was when he was older, whether he was a good person.

One day he came home from school talking about William Jeff's father who was a pilot and had a good car.

Who is my dad? he asked.

It was the one thing I had managed to keep from him, the one memory I kept sufficiently locked up he could not take it.

I moved my hands, miming anything I could think of. Distracted him with photos of astronauts and doctors.

But his question had sent me back to that night in the cornfield. A smell or the sound of husks breaking underfoot; the soft pop of pomegranate seeds between fingers; an arm thrust forward, the skin puckered, the nub of something breaking through: a feather. Then it was gone, the memory. I loved him more then. When I did not remember his conception.

It was too late, though I tried another story on him – a fiction, but no more one than anything else. I spent a month building the story, making it a memory. When I woke in the mornings I would lie in bed and think about it until I believed in it.

When I was younger, I told him, I met a boy. We messed around in the back of his father's car; took our clothes off out by the estuary where we thought no one could see. We had some plans. They were small and simple to carry out. We bought a house in the town we grew up in. He gave me that jug over there as a gift. It was often filled with flowers. The year we knew that you were growing in me, we found there was something, also, that grew in him. I remember the funeral very well.

You don't seem to like that story. Well, what would you have told him when he asked about his father?

It was no good. He understood now where he'd come from. He'd taken the memory of it from me. He changed after that. At night I listened to him foraging through the house. He was taller than me. All body. He had long hands. He looked as if he were made – I always thought this – of scaffolding, rafters. He drew on all the walls and floor. Mostly it was drawings of what he could see. He drew the fridge with the door open and then closed, drew light bulbs hanging from the ceilings of rooms and growing from floors; plug sockets and extension cords. He drew them as if they were creatures in a forest. He drew them more than he ever drew me. I came only as an afterthought: a tiny, out-of-proportion figure in the corners of rooms or emerging from piles of cables.

The stealings carried on. Often he tried so hard not to take anything; curled at the back of the wardrobe, hands pressed over his ears.

But soon I did not remember my name or the names of food or the sense of things. I have memories now I didn't have for ten years. The sight of someone running, I think it is my sister, over a wet field; my father shovelling knuckles of coal into a fire. I had a boyfriend once. I only remembered that the other day.

Towards the end I would hear him crying in the night. He couldn't, he would say, turn bricks into skin, skin into bricks. He did bring home roadkill. Left them sitting for days at a time. As if thinking it was only patience he needed to bring them alive again. When it rained he would stand out in front of the house with his hands held up. Like this. Standing there until it stopped. I was never certain whether he thought he was the one to do that.

I forgot ever giving birth to him; thought maybe I had found him. I forgot the way he was when he was a baby, seeming almost human. I forgot the speed with which he grew, burning through skins. I forgot the way I would sometimes wake and he'd be watching me sleep. The way, the more I forgot to eat, he fed me. He knew how to make the things I liked.

And then, one day, there was a man in my house and I did not know who he was. I was afraid of him. You would have been afraid of him too. I got a knife from the kitchen and I think maybe, if I could, I would have killed him. He looked at me and understood he had taken everything he could and then he left.

*　*　*

112

I listen to the radio. I know about him working the hospitals, opening incubators and lifting out the babies too small to breathe on their own. I get all the local newspapers and each hospital is closer. Some days I check the locks on the doors three or four times. No, I do not know why he is coming back. Only that he is.

It is getting dark out. Do you see? Perhaps you have been here longer than you meant. Maybe you should go.

He sent postcards. In the beginning he sent one a week. In the postcards he used the language he thought he was supposed to. He spoke often about the End of Days. He stopped giving dates when the dates came and went. Near the start he stuck to some of the cults and communes. Those countryside tribes of deep believers living off what scrawny potatoes they could grow; great broods of children. His handwriting was bad and, besides, I was having to learn language anew, picking up stray words. But later, when I'd regained enough to understand, he wrote that it was nice to find someone who believed in him and I knew he was saying that I'd failed in that regard.

I don't think he stayed with any of them long.

After a while he must have got far enough away that I could have all my words again. I began looking at objects and then knowing what they were, replacing the gaps with knowledge. Plant pot, fridge, door. I moved around the house; I went to the shop, picked things up and named them: tin of tomatoes, bottle of milk.

The memories were slower to come. Some of them never came back. But that is to be expected – we all lose memories over time, no? None of us remembers everything. But some of my memories did return, and some of them he gave back to me. Wrote them on postcards: *Do you remember* and I'd realise that, again, I did. He gave me the things he thought were important. He left out anything he was embarrassed about. He was always, as a child, filled with huge bouts of embarrassment, shocking his face full of blood – I remembered that. But I wanted to ask him what happened when I first kissed someone, who it was and how it had gone. This was a thing he would never tell me and I would never ask.

That's when he started sending the photos. In each one he looks like a different person. As if no single body is strong enough to hold him. He wears his hair the way he thinks he is supposed to: long and loose. In the last photo there was a stripe of white, almost a burn, in his fringe.

I wonder often how he would have been if his father were a man. If I am being truthful I do not think of much else. Maybe he would be here now, would have got a job working at the pub or in a shop somewhere. There would be a woman or a man he loved; he would come round and cook me beef stew and dumplings the way I like it and I would enjoy his visits. He would not think he could bring back the dead.

I know who you are though in a moment I will not. It is getting. I do not remember the word. Soon it will be. How easily they go again. There is no loyalty in language. There is no.

THE SCATTERING

A story in three parts

After the Hunt

WELL, IT was done, it was through, it was finished with. The fox sat on its haunches on the floor of the hall and looked up at her. There was a moment, less than that, when she thought she would break it between the ribs or at the neckline. The words she'd given it, his words, would come out easy, as easy as making a baby from clay, easy as swimming to the sea when you had fins rather than legs.

The creature, rusted across the chest, put its head on one side and cracked its mouth an inch or so, panted. She waited for what it would say. A farewell or thank-you or promise of return.

Open the door, the fox said, and though she hesitated she did: then stood and watched until it was gone.

The Scattering

THERE WAS a time she had more than one brother.

He would come to her smelling of the nights he'd grown accustomed to. He would come to her smelling of everything he could get his hands on to drink. Come to her smelling of bonfires and cold sleep. Come to her lit through with a sort of sadness or bruised with unthinking rage. Come to her cut up and proud. She'd wake to the sound of him falling through her window, rising up, grinning hard.

What have you done?

Well, he'd angered in the pub at something mis-said or overheard, winked the culprit – it didn't much matter who – out into the car park, fought them to bleeding on the gravel. But he didn't ever want to talk about that. Instead he'd come to her with a story burning so hot in his mouth he couldn't help but tell it: the house that fell in love with a girl, the girl that starved into a fish. He'd come to her drunk enough to sleep at the foot of her bed the way a cat would, her awake and listening all night to make sure he breathed on through.

So Arch was a different creature than her though they'd come from the same place. She was threaded through with cynicism, taut with anti-belief. He grew still and nervous at the chattering of birds on trees or chimney stacks; worried himself sleepless the summer the cows in the field behind the house milked blood; believed that snakes didn't die only began anew every time they shed their skin.

When the three of them were children Arch almost had her persuaded that nothing was as it seemed. All of them in the long bath and his soggy face near to her ear.

I saw something flying that shouldn't be able to fly. I saw something with skin on the inside. I saw a dog with a personface.

That's bollocks, Marco said. He was on the other side of her, emptying all the shampoo and conditioner bottles into the water. He dug his hands under and upped out a great eruption of foam.

She was younger than them and a girl. They would not fight in front of her. But later she'd find one of them with a bruise the size of their own hand though that was not where it came from. Later she'd catch Arch washing red from his clothes, the colour seeping to clear.

It's tomato juice, he'd tell her if he was hurt enough to fail at imagining. Or he'd say he'd caught something trying to get in the house and he'd stopped it.

Even then, the only thing the boys shared, twelve years old and she not quite eleven, was that they never understood the fear of violence other people had.

And everything anybody said about twins was a lie. They said twins could tell what each other were thinking across the room; could live in one pronoun happily enough and were connected with invisible, pliable bones. Well, if Arch and Marco were tied together they were trying mightily hard to break apart. And if they knew what the other was thinking it was only because they'd beaten it out of them earlier that day.

When tired, their mother said they should have been separated at birth, should have been fostered out to the bears or ferrets because that is where they really belonged. They could feud then, she would say, in the forest where they wouldn't hurt anybody with their aggressions. They could forge wars with animals on each side and flint as weapons and they would not miss anybody: they would forget there ever had been anybody to miss.

Matilda always wanted to say: but they would miss her. They would come back to visit her; bring her the animals too timid to fight their wars; bring her whatever presents the forest gave up. She wanted to tell her mother that sometimes she dreamt of Arch in the forest. There were dead rabbits and birds swinging from the cuffs of his trousers, his face slicked with war marks of black mud, his hands blue and cut from shucking the oysters which had started to grow in the canals at his bidding.

By the time they were teenagers, her friends at school fancied one or the other of them. They were two years above her and wore their scars as if they were medals. She tried to answer her friends' questions fairly. She told them that Marco was a steady guy: could do crosswords pretty well, knew how to cook fish and chips and not much else, played the cello because he'd heard Jacqueline du Pré on the radio and told their mother – he was ten years old but already a bit of an arsehole – that he was pretty certain he could do the end bit better. By nine he knew all the swear words there were to know and used them eloquently.

She told them Arch could outrun a beat-up car; could stand on his head longer than anybody would believe and liked old films with Cary Grant and Katharine Hepburn in them. She didn't tell them that he could hunt an animal clear across the flats or hear a rabbit before it heard itself.

She didn't tell them the only time Marco and Arch wouldn't fight was when they went out hunting the foxes. She kept that to herself. The sight of them tramping off across the back field, walking far enough apart you could think it an accident they went in the same direction. The sight of them coming back an hour or more later, mud on their hands and faces and all over their clothes. Marco would shower straight away and she'd listen to the sound of Arch taking two steps at a time on the way to her room. He'd come in looking smug, lie on the floor at the foot of the bed so as not to dirty her sheets.

Did you have fun? she'd ask. She wanted more than anything for him to tell her about the hunt, about picking up tracks from soil and bent branches. He never would.

I heard a new story, he'd say instead.

There had been incidents with the fen foxes. Horses and sheep attacked; something bad up at one of the farms which started a cull big enough you couldn't hear the sound of them at night for a while. They'd dropped poison into the fox earths, tried to gas them out. They were different from the foxes you got in the cities, those wry, narrow-hipped creatures, caught in alleys, scrounging the bins behind takeaways, eating mice and complacent squirrels. Fen foxes were a bigger, wiser, more knowing stuff of a being. They'd got used to living well and good off fat rabbits and muntjac deer. They were too big for their boots.

There wasn't anything special about either of them except they thought they didn't belong there. But didn't everybody, she'd say while her friends leant back and watched the mudded thighs of the boys playing football on the school field, didn't everybody want to bloody leave?

A couple of times she set one or other of them up. Stood against the door frame of Arch's room, watching him get ready.

Why you wearing that?

She looks like the sort who likes blue.

Well, she isn't.

He worked his fingers through his hair. He wore his T-shirt the way she'd seen James Dean wear his in those films, high at the arms and hips. It fitted him the way it was supposed to. In fact he looked, she thought, entirely the way men did in those old films: hair back and up from his forehead, cigarettes in his tight jean pockets. He didn't belong anywhere real. Certainly not there.

You're wearing too much aftershave.

S'all right, Mattie, I'll take you on a date soon.

He would come home late enough he had to take the drainpipe. She lay listening for him. Was awake when he knuckled on her window. Let him wait. She'd never done it, hadn't lost it; but she knew what the smell underneath the booze was.

He tumbled in, bruised his lip, rose laughing loud enough to show he didn't care.

Cat got your tongue, Mattie?

That was the way he was, she thought, cold from the open window, looking at him lick blood off his fingers: everybody had to know how much he didn't give a shit.

The next day she caught enough to know what had happened (in the field, muddy, lasted about a minute) before her friends saw her listening and shut up fast. Nobody wanted to hear how their brother had given it up.

She didn't stand in Marco's doorway to watch him get ready and he didn't climb her drainpipe to get back into the house. She never understood when people asked how she could tell her brothers apart: they were as different as everybody else was.

When they were in their last year C.E came to the town from America. It didn't take long before everybody knew Marco had set his sights on her. He wasn't coy about anything, didn't have the make-up for that. People said she was playing hard to get because she was from the US, but they all thought he was cute enough for her to at least kiss. C.E was straight up and down and taller than Marco. She wore herself as if she'd had longer than the rest of them to get used to it.

There were stories about C.E and Marco the way there were about everything. Someone said the first time they'd done it was out in that empty horse arena; someone said he'd wanted to wait and she'd not talked him into it; only boiled his blood enough he couldn't bear not to. Someone said he'd wooed her with his cello, carrying it out to her house and setting up shop on the lawn until C.E's father chased him away. Someone else said he'd given 'the cello' to her that first day she was at school, just handed it over as if it meant less than nothing. Someone said they didn't stop fucking for a week, only came out of it on Sunday morning and wandered out from between the trees. A lot of people liked to say they'd seen them, naked or with half-scraps of clothing on, both of them bruised to hell and nearly blind, stopping cars out on the A-road.

People would say what they were going to say.

Matilda grew used to the sound of her brother building to something on the floor of his room as if he thought it would be quieter down there. She never heard C.E. Only caught her coming out of the bathroom afterwards, hair back in place, yellowing marks on her neck and arms.

She grew used to what C.E left around the house, to the thin underwear their mother hooked out the laundry basket, the half-full perfume bottles, the boxes of tampons. And, once, a pack of pills she turned over, thought about, understood only later. Wished she was bodily in that way. Not just made of what you needed to work.

A Saturday. Marco home without C.E for the first time in almost a year. It felt the same as a funeral or wedding. There was a slowness to everything he did. He made them cups of tea ineptly, thin brown lines of water across the counter and floor to the bin, too much milk or not enough, the water barely boiled. He had grown, she thought, to look less and less like Arch. He sat on the floor in front of them all, her mother in the armchair, she and Arch on the sofa.

I've got a job, he said. A fucking good job.

Don't swear, their mother said.

It's on the boats. We've a house, it's all settled. He paused, sucked up a lipful of cold tea, made a face at the taste.

A fucking house, all settled. C.E's dad's given us the deposit for it.

She waited to see Arch and Marco acknowledge the breaking. The place Marco was going, the boats and the harbour, was stretches far, a public-transport feat. One had not been out of town before, nor had the other, and what that amounted to was both of them being in the same place for all their seventeen years. She could not imagine them divided in this way. That day their bodies, tight together, had smashed through the glass door of the chemistry lab. It was a sort of love, wasn't it?

The two of them sat on the gravel, Arch pulling a shard of glass out of his thin arm, leaning across to do the same for Marco.

Often, walking home, she saw Arch and his friends on the stile at the bottom of the field. They had all finished school a year ago, like Marco, but they were still here. Arch had a job working at the butcher's on weekends. Some of them went into the city to work in bars or supermarkets. There was something about them having not moved on she knew was not right. She overheard people talking about it. She sometimes overheard her mother on the phone saying that supporting a son who only worked two days a week was an embarrassment to everybody but him. Her mother would reply in the negative: she could not throw him out, she'd let him ride it a little longer.

He's sensitive under the bluster, she would say when she got off the phone and caught Matilda watching. If I told him to find his own place, to get a proper job, he'd never see us again.

Seeing him there, perched on the wood, legs swinging, she wanted to tell Arch that he could stop now, he didn't need to fight the boys who hung around outside school spoiling for something or go out stalking the shy fen foxes the way he'd done with Marco when he was still there.

Where did you go? she'd ask when he came in through her window, vaulting up and over, good at it now, from sill to floor. What did you do?

Come on, Mattie, he'd say already half out the door, you don't want to know.

Except she did. She was not the age she'd been when she last tagged around after him and he'd bend to do her shoelaces or let her wipe her nose on the sleeve of his jumper. She wanted to show him the blood that came, wanted him to smell the way she smelt after games or when she woke. She did not smell the way she had when all she had to listen to were the stories he told her.

She spent a couple of days thinking of which friend to ask. Asked Becky, who would say yes to most things because she didn't know how to say no; who'd let one of the older girls shave off her eyebrows when they were in year seven.

Let's go to the pub.

Why? Becky said, looking suspicious.

Matilda shrugged.

We're boring. It was the truth. In a town where there was nothing to do they did well at doing nothing.

It felt like anything else. They walked back to Becky's house after school and ate the baked potato and beans her mother made them.

What are you going to wear? Becky's mother said with an excitement that set her stomach tight: she'd not been going to wear anything but what she'd worn to school all day. The three of them went and stood in front of the wardrobe and looked in and when they were done she looked in the mirror at the make-up on her face and thought it would be best to give up then.

Becky's mother dropped them off at the pub and told them to ring when they wanted to come back. It was cold outside. The headlights turned over their faces then disappeared.

OK, Becky said, though she sounded uncertain, tugging at her bra straps.

Matilda wanted to say: never mind, let's just go home and watch a film. She was frightened of opening the door and standing there, frozen, and everybody turning to look at them and he looking too.

Isn't that your sister?

That night he would not come through her window, she thought. He would knock on the door until their mother woke up. He would do this because of how she'd embarrassed him.

She pushed inside and went straight to the bar. She ordered two rum and cokes as they'd decided. There was nowhere to sit so they stood. Becky was talking nervously about something; words came to her. Mainly they were unsentenced, free-floating. She listened to the male voices she could hear behind her, to both sides. At some points she thought she heard words said the way he said them, was convinced it was him until a word would follow in a voice entirely unlike his.

She wondered if he would come up if he saw her. He would, most probably, pretend he had not. She wondered if he would even recognise her from the back. Becky's mother had curled her hair.

A little later she shifted her weight and there was a readjusting in her head that left parts of the room – the bar, the face of the woman next to them, some of the bottles – hanging behind a moment longer than they ought. She'd never been drunk before though she'd always imagined it would feel a little the way it did.

I think – she said, and then Becky took off, small heels clicking. Matilda went after her into the bathroom and stood at the cubicle door while she threw up.

Can you hold my hair?

OK.

When she was done Matilda rang Becky's mother and they waited.

Arch was at the bar. James, one of his friends from school – she recognised the too-long hair and eyebrow piercing – stood next to him.

You all right there, Becky? James said, grinning. Arch didn't say anything.

Matilda went outside with Becky. It was colder than it had been before and there was a creature keening somewhere.

I'll drop you home. Becky's mother was in her dressing gown. She had a hot-water bottle on her lap and the car heating running high.

My brother's here, she heard herself saying. I can go home with him.

It seemed an answer good enough, though she knew, because she knew him, that it was not. Again, the headlights passed over her face and disappeared. She went back into the pub. Got a drink. Went to the big table where he was sat with all his friends. Stood by his shoulder. She would wonder later where she got this bravery from. She'd always thought Arch and Marco had stolen all there was.

He was not speaking, only leaning back to listen. One of his friends was talking, though she could not hear the words.

Matilda, right? a girl with blue in her hair said, leaning her head on one side to look her up and down.

She nodded.

Pull up a stool, Mattie, James said and laughed as if he'd made a joke. She went searching for a stool. It was getting late but the pub was busy enough there wasn't one. She did not want to go back again. To stand there and have one of his friends ask her why she hadn't brought a stool back or suggest she sit on the floor or on someone's lap.

She stood at the bar for a bit. She caught some of the older people looking at her, pretended she didn't see them. She skidded an empty glass along the wood with her thumbnail.

It was a good three miles back to the house. She took off her shoes, did most of it at a run. She thought, as she went, about him doing this same route. He would not run. He had all the time in the world. Don't run, he said when they were younger; they'll see you. She ran and ran until she was damp across her forehead and in

131

her hair. Took the drainpipe. It was easier than she'd thought.

She did not wake up when he came through her window and in the morning he was gone before she got up.

What's wrong with you? her mother said.

She had made them coffee. They were going shopping in the city.

Nothing.

They went and caught the train. They would go to Gap or one of the other places where there was nothing but long-sleeved T-shirts and dresses that went down to the ankle and up to the neck. She might as well wear a hood backwards over her face. She might as well wear a burkha. She wanted to go to that sex shop. She did not know the name but she wanted to go there and come away with a bag which had the name written on it so everybody would know.

At school the next week Becky was angry at her for staying. It was your idea, she kept saying. I never wanted to go.

She knew she should apologise. There were ways for an easy life and that was one of them. There were rules and orders connecting friendships.

Arch was there on the stile with his friends when she walked down the field towards home. She stopped before she got to them. Stopped and looked at the massed group.

He'd been fighting again since the weekend; a cut above his eye, bruised knuckles. Well, they were pikeys, he always used to say. He was like a dog let loose in a pit without knowing nobody was watching.

She walked up. They were smoking.

We're going up to the field. Want to come?

It was not him. One of the other boys – all of them held heavy bags of bottles and cans. He had rings and a lopsided tattoo.

OK.

OK? the boy parodied, rocking his eyebrows.

She shrugged. Yeah.

They'd made a sort of place in the midst of one of the copses of thin trees that were spaced across the flats. There was a fire pit dug into the ground and scattered with beer cans and cigarette stubs. Someone had piled up dirt in meticulous, strange slopes she was confused by until the boy with the tattoo lugged a skateboard from his rucksack, rode a smooth curve, flipping high at the top, smoothing back round. Most of the trees had suffered their damages. As if they'd been coming there for years and years. There were names and symbols and the scoring patterns of unidentified games marked into the bark, reaching up higher than her head.

She stood and watched the slow, almost domestic bustle of them. The girl with blue hair went at the fire, bobbing a little on the backs of her heels, making odd triangular structures out of small sticks and twisted paper, lighting the base of them so they went up strut by strut. Someone else was letting the beer cans float, to cool, in the small, dirty turn of spring just at the edge of the trees. They gave her one and she cracked it down with her thumb and put her mouth to the explosion of warmish foam which bubbled onto her face and down to the ground.

It was light yet. They seemed in no hurry, though she felt she was waiting for something, for a truth or an understanding. They sat around the fire and spoke in pairs or as a whole and now and then one or the other of them would add more wood to the fire so it burnt higher. With her, they engaged in the sort of conversation she felt adults must work through at dinner parties. They asked what she was studying at school and what her plans were for later and what sort of music did she like and had she seen the new January Hargrave film? She tried to answer them in ways she would not normally answer these questions.

So, the boy who'd invited her said: how old are you anyway?

Fifteen.

He whistled and laughed and some of the others laughed too, as if they were knocking thirty rather than eighteen at the most. As if they'd done everything there was to do. She did not understand that: they had never gone further than the nearest city; they had never done anything worth doing.

What you going to study then?

Don't know. Linguistics? she said.

Like, he rolled his eyes, making up words?

She opened her mouth to reply but he wasn't done yet. Something was changing.

Like, the boy was saying, cockcowwhore or –

She looked over the heads of the people opposite, at the sky which was, from the ground up, draining of colour.

Let's play a game, her brother said.

She hadn't heard him talk much. He did something with his head in her direction. It was the first time he had acknowledged her. She was uncertain what it meant: was he asking her to go or asking her opinion on the matter? He finished his drink, tipped the bottle into the centre of the circle and spun it.

It's not hard, someone said when it landed on her. Now you drink.

She thought there must be times you caught yourself learning. Not the places you'd expect or where you were supposed to, but there in the growing chill beneath the trees with the bottle etching its line towards her and her drinking in answer to its tug. She wondered – well, she was drunk – if she'd look back when she was aged through and remember learning how to be drunk by watching her brother.

Later, when James told her she looked good and he wanted to kiss her she let him. Someone whooped a low grunting sound. When she pulled back, wiped a hand across her mouth, opened her eyes, Arch was watching her. She felt the pit of that look – not bad, only considering.

They played a game she did not know and nobody explained. When the bottle landed on Arch he said things that made her redden and the others laugh at her reddening. He'd shrug, swig, grin.

Later he was kissing someone too. He did it lazy-like, one arm looped around, his mouth moving slow. He was thinking on other things. She found herself watching him – not bad, only considering.

Someone spun the bottle again, though the game had flagged, failed. The dark of the tree lids above her coughed to motion. Then James – who'd kissed like a shark, small, fast-moving teeth – was looking at her.

Arch, he said. Dare you to kiss Mattie, and she turned to watch her brother pulling his face back, slipping his arm free.

He came over without much ado. He didn't make a fuss. That wasn't the way he was made. He would never lose face: you could dare him to swing down onto the train tracks and he'd do it, leg over leg and onto the metal runners.

He would never do anything by halves.

His tongue in her mouth quickish and tasting of the hot dog and onions she'd watched him eat. She wasn't pulling back but he had a hand in her hair all the same, holding her firm. It went on. She had her eyes open because she'd forgotten she was supposed to close them. His face was too close to be anything recognisable. She worked out the flat of his nose, stretching away from her cheek. The others were whooping and howling and someone said: a game all the family can play. They were clunking their beer cans on the ground so she could smell the spillage and the wet dirt and he was going on, rhythmic now, as if he were hearing a beat in it all.

She broke and hulked in a mouthful of air and let it cool her insides and he sat back on his haunches like a piss-proud dog and looked at her.

That week she went to drink with them most days.

She finished her exams and did well.

We'll see, her mother said, setting Arch's place at the celebration dinner. But he was only a little late, toeing his shoes off at the door and sliding into his seat and raising his thumbs at her in something both mockery and collusion.

On Christmas Day she stood in the hallway and listened to her mother on the phone to Marco. Her mother did not say much (don't swear, Marco, please) but still – from the little Matilda heard – anybody with half a knowing of what Marco was comprised of could guess what had happened. Matilda wondered what a baby made a little of someone like her and a little of someone else would look like.

*   *   *

She was never certain why Marco's mistake made Arch so angry. She saw him scrapping or heard about him scrapping all that next week, picking fights with anybody who came close enough he could call them out. One of the girls at school, prim with it, said he was out of his league, that play-fighting at school was fine but this was different and everybody in town was tired of his bullshit.

She went back to the fire pit beneath the copses once or twice a week. She dressed carefully, looking down at herself. Marco and Arch looked so like one another, like a mistake doubled across a space. She looked like leftovers, what had come after. She drew, haphazardly, a black line across the rim of her eyelids the way she'd seen his friends do.

Those long nights he was fidgety, could not keep still. She saw the way his friends treated him, with a wariness that normally comes around animals that don't have the language to be reasoned with.

Often he came to the field late, lifted up his T-shirt silently so they could see the fresh marks, the dirty scrapes of blood. He was going further and further afield to pick fights, was taking the train or hitch-hiking to the city to find bars where they wanted it as bad as he did. There were still people who wanted it that bad. She could see his friends growing bored with this show, with his hand reaching for the rim of the shirt, with his thinness coming into view. He would point out the new ones with a pride that made her wonder if he even fought back any more.

Have a drink for fuck's sake, someone would say and the moment would pass. Except she would remember the scratches and bruises. She would remember each new one.

At the end of the year there was a car outside school and C.E was sat in it with one arm hanging out the window though it was near freezing and the other hand banging on the horn to call her over.

Mattie, right? she said, although they'd spent almost a year passing one another in the hallways of the house.

Yeah.

She sat and tried not to look too hard but looked all the same. She remembered seeing C.E in the sports changing rooms, nearly naked, the long telescope of those legs, talking and talking. She wasn't going to stay there. She was there because, second time around, her father had married a British woman. She knew the rest of them would get stuck stocking shelves and getting fat. She wasn't like that.

Except. There she was. She was still carrying a little of the pregnancy weight around her belly and, braless, her breasts were heavy. She was languid the way she had always been, long-bodied in the loose dress, legs a little apart, woollen socks and wellington boots. There were cigarette butts in the ashtray.

They drove out of the car park. Matilda could not think of anything to say.

Is this your car?

It's a friend of mine's. She let us borrow it.

They drove the rest of the way without saying anything.

Walking to the house she listened for the sound of the baby or of Marco and Arch going at it the way they had when they were younger. The house was quiet.

C.E kicked her wellingtons off against the wall and went in. The baby was on the carpet in the sitting room. It wasn't moving much only lying on its back, looking at the ceiling. Her mother was on the floor, not close enough to touch the baby but near enough to see with good detail, knees bent beneath her, one hand holding up her head.

Matilda followed C.E into the kitchen. Marco was there and so was Arch. They were drinking tea. Arch was leant against the counter and Marco was sat at the kitchen table. They weren't talking any.

Hello, Mat, Marco said, one hand around the tight bone of C.E's hip.

Hi.

In the next room they could hear their mother talking to the baby.

What's its name? Matilda said, too loud because nobody was saying anything. Everybody looked at her.

Skyla, C.E said. It's my grandmother's name.

She looked at Arch. He was pale across the face and neck; his mug was full.

Her mother made pasta with tomato sauce. She kept waiting for Arch to make his excuses or just go. She steeled herself to say that she was going with him, that she wanted to go to the field and drink with his friends too. Occasionally the baby would make a huffing sound as if it were bored; otherwise it didn't do much. Sometimes she caught a smell from it, a warm, half-asleep smell.

After dinner, Arch's bony legs were over the side of the armchair and he'd found a beer from somewhere and was drinking it slower than she'd known he could drink beer. She wanted one but didn't know how to ask. He didn't comment on the baby, seemed barely to notice it was there. Occasionally C.E would stand and go and rearrange its clothes or look down at it.

Arch was speaking to her now. You remember Harry, he would say to her. Or: you heard what Sarah said the other night? She was pleased, as if they were plotting a thing. She had a book out because she didn't know what else to do with her hands. Sometimes she looked up and he was watching her that way he did of a time. Not bad, only considering.

Later, Marco and C.E had an argument about something someone had said. It went on a good ten minutes and got louder and louder until they seemed to run out of steam.

Crazy fucking cow, Marco said after a moment.

Quiet, idiot.

Marco talked a bit about the boats. He wasn't used to them, he said, had thrown up the first five or six times and they'd said he wasn't made for it and should work at the pub. He was, he said, better now, could manage a fair swell without losing his breakfast. He scoffed about a burnt-out lighthouse and the superstitions the sailors had which he had to pretend he held with. C.E didn't say much more.

You going to stay there? Arch said.

Marco shrugged. Don't know. Maybe.

Sounds a shit-tip.

Not as shit as here.

Give it a rest, C.E said, and Matilda thought that, though she might have birthed something up that looked like one or other of the boys, she didn't know the first thing about the danger of them.

It's all right, Marco said, sounding amiable enough, don't get your pants in a fucking twist.

It was dark outside. The baby had fallen asleep on the carpet with its limbs splayed, not moving. I'll do it, her mother said when C.E moved to take her upstairs. She did not come down and it was different without her there. Arch came back with four beers and handed them out without it seeming much of a thing to do.

I haven't pumped, C.E said, and gave hers to Marco, who drank both of them at the same time as if it were a joke everybody had known was coming.

You remember that time we sucked all the petrol out of Mrs Williams's car? Marco said, holding his beer up.

Yup.

Did she know it was you? C.E said.

Everybody knew it was us, Marco said.

Arch drank down a gulp of beer and looked at Matilda. She wondered what he wanted; whether he wanted her to stop whatever was going to happen, whether he'd always, really, wanted her to stop it. She waited for him to give her a sign. She was not certain what she would say, only that she would muster something. Remind him he'd told everybody he'd go to the pub.

Eventually Arch looked away, said: you remember when we used to track foxes?

I thought you said he loved animals. C.E's voice was loud.

Marco shook his head. It wasn't like that. We never killed one. It wasn't about killing them. We'd just follow the tracks until we caught up with it, chase it for a while and then let it go.

What's the good in that? C.E was talking loud still, as if to cover something. Matilda could feel Arch wincing at the sound of her voice.

You wouldn't understand. You never do anything unless there's an exact point set out for it.

She waved a hand at Marco. No, I just don't see the point in chasing an animal like that.

He didn't see the point in hurting an animal – Marco rolled his chin at Arch. We could have got close enough to skin it with our hands but he would have skinned me first.

C.E laughed and stretched so you could see the slight handhold of flesh between her T-shirt and jeans. Matilda watched them watching her.

You couldn't have got that close, she said, stretching still, not really looking at either of them.

Foxes are cleverer than that, at least the ones we have back home. You couldn't even get within spitting range, otherwise you would have come home with a fox brush. Boys like you always lie. It's all you're good for.

Marco watched her carefully. He looked like he'd never seen anything who wore her skin the way she did. You're wrong, C. Right, Arch?

Arch didn't say anything.

They're easy to track. Foxes. You just have to know how and fucking go about it really quietly until you're close enough and then you get loud and they lose all their cleverness and you can chase them down.

Bullshit, she said and Marco downed the last dregs of the beer from both cans and laughed at her with his head resting back against the chair.

Well, we can show you.

Show me what?

She turned her face between them.

Show you how it's done.

You idiot. It's dark.

Marco shrugged.

You're bluffing, she said and jabbed a finger in his direction.

We can show you, can't we, Arch?

She knew then there was nothing she could do about it and got up to put on warm socks before they could leave without her. When she came back down the front door was open and Arch and Marco were stood in the square of light, smoking and not talking. Marco looked her up and down and dropped his cigarette into the dimness, moving a foot to cover it.

You're not coming. I don't know what you think you're doing.

She looked at Arch. She wanted to nudge him, tell him she wanted to be there. She had to be there. Didn't she?

He didn't say anything, only let out all his breath, and Marco laughed and said: go upstairs and you can watch out for us coming back.

She didn't go or say anything, only stood waiting until C.E came out of the bathroom with a big jumper on and her hair tied up and said: all right then, and the three of them went out leaving the door swinging, and she watched them until they hit the road and it was too dark to tell their bodies from the rest.

The Hunt

A T THE wake people talked without reserve. Nobody much believed Marco. Some said it was an accident, Arch slipping and falling; Marco making up a story out of grief or madness. Others disagreed. Everybody had seen them as children, out wrestling in the road, ignoring the cars. And older, bleeding before they'd barely begun, fighting with a sort of joy. A play-fight out of control, someone said.

It was the foxes, she heard Marco saying loudly into a room talking mostly on him. I told you all. It was the foxes. There was a silence. Everybody had a plate with food on, salad and spring rolls and a quiche one of the teachers at the school had made. A lot of Arch's friends were there, ones she'd known from the place under the copses, and they were drunk.

Later, when she went up to the bedroom, Marco was there, on the bed, both hands under his head, muddy boots on the duvet.

What are you doing in here?

He shrugged.

Mattie. Mattie, he said, as if he'd only just realised on her being a living thing at all.

She waited for him to tell her the truth. To say they'd worked it all out; they'd decided on a good, last fight and there it was. Arch wanted it this way.

One of them took him, Marco said after a moment. One of the foxes. I reckon one of them is carrying his

146

soul or whatever around inside it at the moment. You believe in that?

He didn't wait for her to answer.

I never did. Always thought he was talking bollocks. All those stories about them.

She wanted to take a hold of him. By the shoulders or by the ruff of his hair. Shake him and shake him. Tell him he didn't need to lie to her, he shouldn't lie to her.

He looked at her as if he knew all the things she was thinking. You believe me, don't you?

She'd been sleeping in Arch's room since he'd died. Sometimes she woke in the night and the smell of him was so thick, so cloying and heavy on her face that she was certain he'd come back all on his own. He would be standing at the foot of the bed, one hand holding up the rim of his T-shirt so she could see the marks the foxes had made on his belly and chest. He would show them with a proudness as if to say that all the other fights had only been leading up to this one. Sometimes she woke to the dull thrum of all the words he'd ever said beating a new sort of pulse through her head. Sometimes she woke with the feel of his tongue pushing against the roof of her mouth and thought – if only he pushed hard enough – he could give her the words.

That night she lay and thought about when they were younger. Out playing in the garden, they would see one on the field. The flush of it, paused at the hedge line or nose down, hunting in the ruts. Marco would shrug, go back to digging. Arch would run to the fence, duck under, go streaking across the field in pursuit. Come back ruddy-cheeked, sheepish.

We saw a fox, he'd tell their mother as soon as he could. Spend the rest of the day talking about it until Marco got bored enough to rile him into fighting.

Later, older, coming up her drainpipe, the stories he told were always threaded through with that slim shape. As if they'd climbed into his gullet, infected his words. But the stories had changed: fen foxes who'd been people once and grown out of themselves easy as taking off one jumper and putting on another. Foxes that carried the dead inside them. Foxes who would speak if only you could make them.

The next day she went looking for the fox that had him.

It was early, dark. She went straight across the field out the back of the house, slipping in and out of the damp, tractor-cut furrows. It did not feel the way it was supposed to. It felt only that her brother was dead and she was out walking in the early morning.

She walked hard, fast, tripping forward. A little light grew on the straight line in front of her. She heard the pylons before she saw them, their low, tuning-fork buzz. In the distance there were cars passing. This land was deceptive: they were miles away. She kept on.

Later there was that laughing bark in the distance. She turned to listen. Started in that direction. Then the sound cut from behind her. She turned and turned. Settled on the same way as before. Kicking at the high grass at the edge of the field. It would be light soon anyway and then it would be no good.

She had reached, without realising, the copse with the fire pit and the soil skateboard ramps. She went into the black beneath the thin wind-breaker trees, waded into the fire pit to search for half-burnt beer cans with the toe of her wellington. Went to the river and bent down to squint for any left behind, bobbing in the water.

There was something under the trees, just before the slope that ran up to the field. A fox caught by the foreleg in a trap. It took her half an hour to get the trap open. The fox panted and made a high sound she had not heard from the ones who used to mate or hunt rabbits out the back of the house. Its leg was caught good. She wrenched and forced. It snapped its jaw at her, lunging open-mouthed as far as the trap would allow.

When it was done the fox started up the bank and she gave a gentle tug on the leash she'd attached around its neck and it fell back and looked at her with an astonishment that almost made her let it go then and there. Her hands were bleeding.

She dragged the fox on. The lights of a car came over the rough, holed concrete road. The pylons went on and on in the sheer beam of it. She wrestled the fox hedgeways, out of the road, but it got its mouth pretty sharpish round her wrist and bit down. The car rolled on and then stopped. She could see nothing of the driver but their gloved hands on the wheel. She could smell the fresh rage of the fox, the pissed-off stench of it. The car got moving again, flashing its red tail lights in farewell, and she thinking there can't have been many other places where people would mind their business the way they did in the fen.

It was almost morning, a thin wash of colour. She could see the lights on in some of the houses they passed, could hear raised voices. They were almost there when the fox sat down and would not move. She strained at the leash, it tightened its neck, stretched its head away. Its leg left patterned red on the road. It panted evenly, looked away from her at the whitening stretch of land. She came at it with both arms out, upped it onto her hip, held its snout closed tight. Stumbled on.

In the sitting room she could see the back of Marco's head over the top of the sofa, could smell the cigarette he was drawing on.

Where you been, Mattie? he called out into the hall.

She almost told him. I think this is the fox that has Arch. I think this fox is Arch. She was uncertain how she would say it, only that she was certain.

Just out walking.

There was an inconvenience to keeping a fox het up where it didn't want to be. Her feet were black with scat and piss. She had bandaged its leg up the best she could but it needed changing every day. It had taken her pillows apart with its teeth and was working on the duvet. It yipped and growled and stank.

Food was a problem. Sometimes she caught her mother in front of the fridge; face lit yellow, looking in at the emptiness. Marco, staying on to keep them company, sat on the sofa and ate pot noodles.

She tried it on cat food. It would have none of that. Ignored, too, the leftovers she smuggled up. There was a flow of dinners deposited on their doorstep. Nobody ever knocked. This was a place where people understood the possibility of bad luck being passed on and kept clear. Still. There was a lasagne most days and often a shepherd's pie. Without it there would have been no food at all. Marco ate a lot, great platefuls, seconds. Her mother none at all. Matilda brought up what was left in the dish it had been cooked in, slid it across the floor. The fox did not even put its nose down to smell, only looked at her over its disdainful narrow snout.

She waited for her mother or Marco to come bursting in. At night she heard one or the other of them pacing the front of the house. She met her mother in corridors, coming out of the bathroom, at the foot of the stairs. When Matilda spoke she looked at her the way people did at parties, failing to remember a name.

She tried the fox on cuts from the butcher's. The cheap bits of chicken, chunks of stewing beef. The fox watched her drop her offerings on the floor, stepped back a couple of paces. Then leapt onto the windowsill, where it was most of the time – looking out. She was sure she could see, through the dulling-out pelt, the scaffolding of its ribcage. The room started to smell: her mother had the heating on high all the time now.

One of the little Farrow sisters had put the male hamster into the female hamster's cage and now was out on the roadside as penance, selling the small, furry creatures by the handful. She carried five of them back in the box. Let them free into the room. Did not stay to watch. There was not much noise. Only the sound of the fox padding down from the windowsill.

Later she brought in, hopefully, the leftover roast chicken someone had dropped off. It did not even lift its nose up. Did not even open its eyes. She knew now there was no use in feeding it anything dead.

So the next morning she went walking up to one of the farms, bartered a chicken from a tired-looking woman in jeans. Smuggled it into the house. The fox was waiting, shifting back and forth as if it were dancing something new for her. She held the chicken up by its legs. The chicken was very still. The three of them watched each other.

You can have it if you speak.

The fox's eyes came onto her face, mouth panting open.

You remember the stories?

II

BIRTHING STONES

S HE GAVE her name at the door. The table was in the middle of the room, beneath one of the vent lights. Emma stood until they moved her to a new one in the corner. Handed back the wine list without looking. Ordered a glass of Kalyra, bent to push off her tight shoes.

She was early and she thought (his syllables on the phone, the placing of his punctuation in the message when they organised the date) that he was the late sort. It did not matter any. Sometimes nobody turned up and she ate anyway and did it at her own speed like it was what she meant to do all along. Sometimes she wondered, holding the prongs of the fork against her tongue, if they'd come into the restaurant and seen her. Maybe the light was falling wrong onto her face, or she was turned to a bad angle, or her make-up was day-worn and they'd changed their minds and left. She would eat her pearl-barley risotto or polenta and squash until it was gone. Order a glass of dessert wine or coffee and sit until that was too.

A couple came and sat at a nearby table. They looked like an advert; he older, tight inside his shirt; her thin arms and boned shoulders, hair pushed up at the front of her head. He took the wine menu and looked at it.

The photo on the website showed the man she was going to see tonight standing on a canal boat somewhere. Tanned, elbows pistoning out from his body like a boxer. Stood like a boy on a road trip posing with his friends. He had the look of one of those university men whose hair shuttered away to white when they were twenty-four and who wore it well. He reminded her of a badger. He was loosening a little around the hips and ribs. The first time they spoke on the phone he told her the name of the boat like it was a code word.

He was late now, not by much but there it was. He worked in the city somewhere. On the phone he'd talked, flirting, about a wine bar he thought she would like. They could sit outside under the burners and drink Kir and afterwards he would put her on the train. Or he would not. There was a gap behind everything with him that she enjoyed. Always the sense that if she pushed down she would come upon a meaning, waiting.

I can show you where I work, he'd said.

There had been reasons she'd given for not wanting to go to the city. Something about an early shift. She'd talked about the restaurant she wanted to take him to.

The food was good there. They drove the fish in every morning. They served crab. He said she sounded like she'd taken other men there. She thought about it. Decided she liked the undertone of jealousy.

She wanted to tell him the truth. A gift he'd not asked for or wanted but one she would give to him all the same. The truth was she wanted to go to the city and sit beneath the burners with hands cold enough she would induce him, eventually, to take her fingers into his mouth. Only this was not a possibility. She was limbed to the ground. To that place, this town. Like a root. Planted in.

She caught the waiter's eye. Went to the bathroom in the absence between one glass and another. The joints between her fingers were sore from the actions of the night so far: holding her wine glass, bending around the menu. She held them beneath the tap's flow. Wet her face and neck. Felt cracked and parched; dredged up and left too long in the midday. Dried herself on the hand towel – left a smudge of colour – reapplied the powder.

At the table she broke one of the rolls, filled its centre with oil and ate. When she was younger she would watch people through the windows of restaurants or on park benches. The shapes their mouths made, the fence posts of teeth around a sandwich, the length of fork gulleting in. Coming out clean. She would never wake with a hunger or eat to fill a hole inside her. But she'd taught herself the pleasure of it: eating.

She could learn new things, but she was unchanging. She was unchanging and, though she knew everybody felt that way, everybody else was not. Most days, at the hospital, she'd place her hands on their oddities: a distended abdomen, the outcrop of bone from a break. The great rocks of flesh rolled in towards her; the smoker's concrete lungs, the young girl's teeth eroded away. The strain of organs against skin. She could stand the bulimic, the obese, the iron deficient, the alcoholic and drug users. The woman who'd unsighted herself with a clothes pin. The overzealous father: two cigarette burns against his boy's arm. But when they left – the ease with which they went from place to place shook and hurt her. They did not think of boundaries, of lines. Didn't need to. She did not allow herself to watch them going, loaded clumsily into cars, limping towards the bus stop, emptied out of wheelchairs.

She drank her glass to the halfway mark and ordered soup for her starter. The waiter asked if she wanted the other plate and cutlery cleared away.

He's often late. Don't worry.

The man at the next table was talking, not eating much. She imagined him running along the canal in the morning, thinking – while he ran – of the marks the running made, the answering pressure of wine and too much red meat.

Her starter came. She thought about what she would say when he arrived. She thought he still would. She would stand to meet him, let him kiss her on the cheek, let him say his apologies. He would be dressed in a suit; his tie off and the top few buttons of his shirt undone. He would ask what she was drinking and order her another and then order himself something different. He would look at her across the table, maybe compliment her on her dress or say something about the way she looked very like her photo and that was a good thing. She would let him say those things.

They could talk about films, yes, and books, maybe, and travel and wine. He would hold her wrist often across the table. She would move her legs across his calves. An accident.

What they were really talking about was, firstly, how much they didn't care about the food or the wine or the way they'd dressed themselves. What they were really talking about, secondly, was the way they wanted it to go when they were done with the meal. What they were really talking about, thirdly, was whether they could bear to set something rolling between them that might never end.

She smiled at the waiter and he came over.

I might as well order. It will serve him right.

Do you know what you would like?

What do you think will make him most jealous?

He flicked open the menu and held it so they could look.

He'll regret it if he walks in and sees you eating that.

He will. He can eat when we get home.

And another glass?

Yes. Please.

She wondered what her mother would have done in her situation. She did not think she would have left. Maybe when she was younger, fleeing, but not later. Later, older, she would have sat and drunk and eaten her food at her own pace. Perhaps her mother was one of those women you saw eating alone anyway, papers in front of her and more often holding a pen than a fork. She wanted to say it to someone. Sometimes she wanted to lean across the table and take them either side of the face with her hands and tell them she cared nothing at all about their views on politics or religion. She didn't care what they thought of any of it. She wanted to explain to them that she had a secret; that they could never even imagine the secret she had and that it made everything they said meaningless. There were times she wanted to say it so badly it would howl out if she opened her mouth.

She knew, because she'd practised, where she would begin: my mother wanted a baby more than she wanted anything else.

He would ask her out of politeness to tell him more. He would owe her that much. She would tell him because he was late. She imagined holding the fort at parents' evenings and violin recitals. He'll be here soon. He's on his way.

The duck came. Splayed and pink. She cut straight down into it and ate the first piece.

She would tell him there was always a way she imagined it. The way it was at the beginning. Her mother trying everything she could. The gathering needles, the phone calls to the doctor, the books. Her mother would not adopt. Other women could shear themselves open for a child with nothing of them inside; she would not. Wikipedia open and her mother drunk enough to follow the mythic commands. Her mother would remember only shards of what she'd done that night: head-standing against the wall till she fell, washing her hands and face in vinegar, writing prayers or promises (remembering only fragments of words: please, girl, never) and burning the paper till it flew. At the hospital they cut the swallowed stones out of her mother's gut, asked what she meant by it. She would not tell them. Only took the pebbles home in her pockets, smooth enough to skim.

She laid her knife and fork down. She worded in her mind the message she would send to him. Not when she got home but the next day, after her shift. Not seeming angry or even much disappointed; only with the meaning of what he'd missed buried behind the words.

No – he would come. She would order pudding, a coffee. He would come while she was finishing. She would not look up for a moment though she would know he was there. He would know that she knew.

Let me pay. An apology, he would say. And, though she did not ever allow anyone to pay for a meal outright, she would let him. And maybe she would punish him a little. He was not the one. Maybe she would tell him that.

What one?

She would shrug. You are not right.

Because I'm late?

She would shrug again.

He would put her coat around her shoulders. They would both listen to her heels on the floor as they left. In his car he would lay out his excuses. And she would remain only lukewarm, would say: my mother had distractions like you.

Is that so?

Yes.

She thought on them sometimes. The distractions her mother must have allowed herself. Running tracks deep into the fields in the mornings, going early to work and leaving late, taking cases home with her and spreading them on the low, dark-wooded coffee table. At weekends she would not sleep in late or watch films in the evenings. It was important there were no gaps for thinking or spare moments for thoughts to slip in.

All the same there must have been times the thoughts came in anyway, butting up before she could ward them off. She supposed it was mostly when her mother let the men come: another lawyer at her firm, a man younger than her she met on the train, the husband of a woman she once knew. Waking up after it was done and looking down at them and them being almost like something she'd given birth to. And then the thought was there. Whether she wanted to or not.

But she settled down enough to have you. Didn't she? he would say.

He'd put the radio on and then turn it off again. She'd take her shoes off and leave them in the footwell.

Yes. She had me.

The decision must have taken in her mother like a seed settled in. She had imagined it enough times she was certain there was no other way it could have happened. Her mother wore a hood, went far out enough from any roads that it was lighting up by the time she got back, hands and cheeks cracking with mud lines. She filled two buckets and the washing basin from the sink.

Fen mud was not like the mud forced to yield crops in other places. Darker than that and wetter and the first child formed on the kitchen table was something of the same, a hunched figure leaking away. She made two of them. Slapping heads onto shoulders, rolling legs thin, fixing bulbous hands into place. Their heads were heavy blocks, features done quickly in the last seconds before she gave up, ears lopsided, eyes slitted with the end of her key, mouths a studious line.

If the man asked her then, busy hands, barely listening, about the years between conception and that night in his car she would not tell him. The surgeries and the word-finding and the days she could not remember because she'd cut them out from her thinking. Watching strangers' mouths to see how to shape words; trying on names from books in the library until one fit. And earlier than that. He could ask but she would not tell him about being more field than human.

She thought little about the other clay child, destroyed then and there, her mother's weight bearing down onto its head. Not what her mother wanted – something barely human at all.

That's a nice story. He would move her hand to his belt buckle.

The waiter came and took her plate away.

How was it?

Very good. Thank you.

Great. Would you like anything else?

Remind me of the puddings.

He went through them. She was tired – she was how she imagined tiredness must feel. She put her hands, not thinking of the waiter standing there, to her stomach and tried to feel the weight of the food.

All right, just the bill I think.

She paid. Put her shoes back on. Went to the bathroom and wet her face and hands again.

At the door, putting her coat on, she recognised him. She thought maybe he would not see her.

*　　*　　*

On hot days she heard the internal crackings of her baked insides, felt the make-up run from her clay skin. Sometimes at night she woke imagining the death of her half-formed twin, the way hands, limbs, face, ears, torso, turned back to only mud before she could crawl away. Sometimes at night she remembered the trail of herself she left behind on the walls and floors of that house. She would not tell you if you asked.

Once she went to a bookshop to buy *Madame Bovary* and saw something curling the woman's mouth as she served her: shock or disbelief. A knowing.

Once she'd got on a train going away from that place. She should have known better. Her mouth mudded thick as road tar, skin began dusting away. Shifting, she struck the nub of her finger against the window and saw the carefully shaped nail crack off. The skin beneath was the same dark as the earth. She looked out at the flats, the washes, the threat of braided rivers.

The ground gave its message easy enough. She could leave but the lack would crumble her away the further she got. They would sweep her out of the train carriage at the final stop. Think nothing on it.

Emma. He was standing at the door, looking at her. He said her name the way she thought he might. The loosening at the end. I'm so sorry.

They went out into the street. He holding his jacket, cheeks a little flushed like a boy's. She could smell the earth, rough and thick from a day's rainfall. They stood awkwardly in the dimness of a closed shopfront. She knew the way his hands would feel in her hair. She readied the words in her mouth.

THE CULL

O N WEDNESDAY she left the washing-up in its piles
in the sink. Went out to the field. The men's backs
were to her, arms folded over ribs, looking at the horses.
Joe Lloyd the vet wasn't there. That was how she knew
they weren't looking at the injuries: the shaved areas where
Joe had stitched the skin closed, the sores around legs
and hocks, jagged stripes across bellies.

The bay, one of them said.

Not that one.

Which?

The old one, next to the grey.

He turned, looked at her. She flattened her stomach
against the fence, lowered her chin.

On Thursday they brought the hooks down from town,
drove them into the walls of the old arena. She felt she
was listening to it all afternoon. Peeling the potatoes,

plucking the chicken bare – trying not to do it to that low-strung beat or look out the window every time they came out to drag in another bag. There were more hooks than there were foxes in the county. The first time there'd only been one and now there were more, but could there really be that many?

By Friday she'd fed them for every meal, the men who'd come from the villages to help, and though she was tired enough to sleep at the table she couldn't sleep at night. The two of them would not talk about it, but she knew he could not sleep either, knew by the way he flipped back and forth. He said single words that she tried to crease into sentences, though it creased to morning before they formed.

She heard enough in the loose swing of the kitchen door to know they would wait for the weekend to finish, wait for Sunday to go through itself, and then they would put the horse in the arena away from the rest.

She knew also from remembering the first time. The way there was a building-up of something nervous and snapping until that night when there was no way they could wait any longer. That time it was a dog, a stray dragged into the barn by its scruff. She never saw the animal, only heard the sounds it made and then the silence, but she'd crept down and looked out the kitchen window and seen the rays of light pitching into the black mouth-hole of the barn and the blurred shapes of the men leaning on car bonnets. She had seen the guns spark off above the trucks but the passage of the bullets into the barn was lost and she had only imagined the cleaving of the air.

In the mornings she carried out boxes of empty bottles, at night she woke to hear their voices raised in protest, argument or merriment. There were only four or five men but they made noise enough for more. The vet was not there – they spoke of things he would not have cared for – and she did not know the names of the others.

Each night she was woken by the sudden bursts of them starting up their cars to drive home and would lie, listening to the sound of him up the stairs, the drunken rest he took halfway. On Friday night he put his balled fists beneath her legs, put her on the floor at the foot of the bed, bent low as though he was going to fall.

On Sunday there were men in the yard out front all day. There were more than before, coming and going, in and out. She made cups of tea in a daze. Burnt the beef brown, undercooked the potatoes. They did not notice, crowded knees and elbows in at the table, slopped their glasses full and then full again, talked loudly. Horses, sheep and cows were being attacked from the Ridgefield's buildings to the start of the coastal farms; a child had scars from the side of its neck up to missing an eye; nobody would keep chickens outside. All the same, this was different from sitting in the pub and talking about the number of birthed cows or the firmness of corn heads. And it was better than talking about a single animal, probably mangy from rabies and on a spree, the way it was the last time. This was something, anyway.

That night, after she'd washed up, she was tired enough to sleep. Was woken later by the cold wash of air coming from the open window, tried to get up and close it. There was a sudden weight on her chest. Held her breath. Then it was gone, and she was throwing pillows aside, looking for the slick body, whatever that weight had been, flicking the light on to show the corners of the room. Only when he stumbled up, took her wrists and held them did she see there was nothing there, and think perhaps there never had been.

He pushed his mouth against her shoulder, pressed his teeth into her skin. This was what it had done to him, the late-night talks, the fast slicks of activity across the farm, the bite marks on the fetlocks.

She woke early that morning. He was still asleep. She lay and looked at his back. Once when they first met in the city, they took bottles of beer to a park, sat on the uprise of a hill. Where I come from, he said, there aren't any hills at all. She made jokes at that, told him that was clear if he could call what they were sitting on anything other than a pimple. He didn't laugh much at that, though he'd been laughing at her jokes all evening, only swilled the bottle up and took a gulp big enough to lessen it by half. The land was in him; he was born with the flats reflecting in his pupils. Even feeling the small bushel of something she felt for him that night was enough to hold her to that place for ever.

She got up without waking him. By the front door she put on her shoes and coat. Crossed the yard, skirting the puddles. At the door to the arena she paused, looked back at the window of their bedroom. She expected to see him there, looking at her.

Seeing the house and fields and barns the first time, she'd been confused as to what the arena was for: a square building with a swing gate. That was until the summer came and she watched them breaking the horses beneath the high corrugated roof. After the animals were broken enough to ride they never stayed long, only given time to grow stocky around the hocks and then off to a riding school or as some child's first pony. Except nobody would buy a horse so mauled that it looked as though you beat it.

She could hear the horses in the stables now. There were chains on the stable doors and Greg Lowe's dog lying outside. She'd heard them debating it in the kitchen, how the foxes got in though some nights three men stayed up late to watch and some nights there were four dogs there. One of them, she didn't know his name, was derisive of their doubting, said foxes were getting into houses, into locked bedrooms; that their barn wasn't much of a challenge. All they were doing was digging under and in. They'd netted the floor. She had spent a weekend sewing the teeth-torn nets whole, though they wouldn't use them for that again.

She went into the arena. They had raked the sand clean of foot – of hoof prints – so she left her own solidly on the walk to the middle. In the centre there was a stake hammered down into the ground with a metal ring bolted to one side. On the walls the hooks were spaced out evenly, going from a little above her head to her knees; three hooks, then along, and then another three. She caught her finger on the end of one, pressed to see it whiten the skin.

When she went back inside, toeing off her shoes at the door, he was at the kitchen table, doing up his boots. She didn't say anything and neither did he. She made coffee and toast, put them in front of him and sat opposite, drinking hers. Thinking of the hooks on the wall, of the stake dug into the sand: she felt famished, and when he didn't move to eat she took three pieces of toast and had them in quick succession. And thinking, then, about afterwards – the post fallen and half buried under sand that is hot and wet; nothing but pieces left over: fur and bone – made more toast and ate that too.

When are they coming? she said.

He brushed the empty toast plate towards her.

Aren't there any eggs?

No, she said, they're all gone.

He spent the morning in the kitchen, at the table, not doing anything, only sitting or asking for more coffee.

Then he cleaned the stalls out, reappearing with wheelbarrows full of muck to empty onto the heap. That only took two hours. Then he was back at the table, pushing toast crumbs into lines with a finger. She put the radio on.

At lunchtime she made him a sandwich. He ate half and she, nervous and ravenous, ate the rest standing over the sink. He stayed there for the rest of the day, now and then pouring himself glasses of water, now and then going upstairs to the toilet, now and then turning the pages of the local newspaper. She got nothing solid done, only half doing anything and then forgetting to finish it. The feeling of it was like the feeling of something else, so when he went to the sink for another glass of water she couldn't help it: put her hands onto the tops of his thighs.

What are you doing?

She didn't answer, cupped her fingers around his legs.

They'll be here soon.

She didn't say anything, pressed herself lengthwise along the back of him, felt the rough burr of energy making her hands shake.

She reached round, fumbled at the catch of his belt. His hands were restraining for a moment, at her wrists, and then gone. She pulled the belt undone, chucked the button free, pushed the zip down.

By the time she was up on the sink and the shaking in her hands was bridging down the rest of her, there were men in the yard shouting for him. She felt him speed himself up, watched the tension in the side of his face;

watched him thinking about afterwards: doing up his trousers and belt, sitting to put his boots on, going out the door, into the barn and fastening the head collar on the horse. It was ruined for her, so that when he was actually doing all these things and she had rearranged her clothes, washed her face and spat into the sink, the bud of fearful energy was worse than ever and there had been none of the release she'd hoped for.

She went outside. Trucks and cars in the yard, more than there had been all week. A dog jumped up at a window as she walked past. In the backs of each vehicle were the heavy farm guns. His – she recognised the smooth clean of it from his working on it at the kitchen table – was leaning against the wall of the stables. The arena gate had been swung open and she could see their shapes moving inside. It was not quite dark yet but it was getting there. She went and stood by the door. She couldn't see much, only heard their quiet voices.

When she moved inside the arena, stood with her back against the wall, she could see better. The horse was tied to the stake in the middle. The men grouped loosely round it. He was beside the head, his fingers looped under the head collar. When they cut the horse – once along its neck, once on each side of its stomach, once on its face – he held on, though the horse was making a high sound and throwing the back of its body around.

She thought she would be able to smell the blood as it went down the sides of the animal and into the sand but she couldn't. She wondered if this was the way it was the first time, when it was only a dog they were cutting and only one fox they were trying to catch.

The bedroom was hot as a flat rock left in the sun. Outside the men were quiet and the dogs in the trucks did not bark. She lay counting for a sleep that would not come. She was waiting for the gunshots but they did not come.

She went barefoot down the stairs, through the kitchen and outside and they did not hear her. It was dark enough there were only shadows of shapes: men by each truck, resting their arms and guns on the bonnets and looking towards the arena. Passing by she could smell the rank sweat of them. She tried to pick out the one that belonged to her by the smell of him and the sound of his breathing; could not. A man walked past her and she bent against the shade of the barn and he did not see her.

At the door to the arena she waited for a sudden shout or hands pulling her back. There was nothing. It was too dark to see anything. She stepped inside, and moved slowly around the wall, keeping her back tight against it, then went forward, shifting the toes of one foot into the sand and then the other, hands held out to either side. When she touched something – wet and warm – she pulled away fast and felt the horse's fear and put her hands over her face. Only it did not come at her and she put a hand back out and then the other and moved close enough to touch the blood. The horse's nose came heavily down onto the cup of her arm. They stood like that for a long time. There was no sound from outside and she wondered how long they would wait.

The horse was drawing in long, harsh breaths through its nose, and then she felt a jolt in its sides. When she looked she could see the pulled-back whites around its pupils and then she realised she could see other things: the shape and size of the barn, the shape of the horse's head and body, her own hands as she held them up.

The horse made a sound the same as when the men had cut it and pulled back hard so the rope burnt across her arm and when she looked she could see the fox too. It was standing a few feet away, its head turned to one side, its body angled. It stood there and looked at her and she looked back.

Behind her the horse jerked back and forth, the noise of the rope and the head collar and the smell of the animal's fear, and she wondered if there were more, skirting in around the walls the way she had, feeling their sides against the wood, crossing towards her.

She did not look away from the fox and, though already there was movement growing and growing around them, the fox did not look away either.

THE LIGHTHOUSE KEEPER

T HE FIRST time she saw the fish she was leaning out
from the side of the crusted rocks at the base of
Bovary, reaching for the umbrella she'd seen from up top.
The fish came cresting up. It was narrow-bellied when it
rolled to curse her, the dark flesh sliding off to white
before it reached the stomach; the eyes, when it lolled
frontwards and ogled her, round as marbles. She stood
watching the lope of it, the way it surfed up to jaw word-
lessly at her.

Inside she hooked out the fish guide from its shelf, laid
it down on the sofa, and flicked through the pages. There
were all the fish you could have and some she thought
there couldn't possibly be, even right out there in the
mess. Trout and marlin and shoals of sardines with bones
small enough to eat whole. There weren't any fish that
looked like that one, not in these waters and not with
that body; none, she thought, slim enough to fit through

the cracks in boat hulls, or long enough to turn back and watch their bodies coming after. Fish like that could breathe air and travel on land – of that she was relatively certain.

Towards the end of the light shift she went to the walkway up top and the sky was going fast with the air coming in big open-mouthed bursts. A storm was unbuckling itself from somewhere. The radio would start going soon and she'd be pitched down beside it, no time to think of the fish or anything else. She pulled the slicker up to her nose.

When the dark shift was over she walked down to the beach. It was a spit of sand, a long tide-walk running from land to water with the lighthouse at the very tip, and she'd salvaged well from it before, the lighthouse busy with shelves and drawers filled with leftovers. A storm like that would normally leave plenty: bottles and plastic bags but treasures too; water-cleansed seal skulls, silver rings whittled thin. And, once, a heavy round clock too watered through to count time.

Today there was nothing to find. She walked back up to the lighthouse, paced the rocky base in a widening circle to check, went down with her hands into the puddles, kicked clods of wet muck aside.

It was the fish that had done it. She'd known it on the walk back to Bovary and on the walk up the stairs and she knew it all day and it stopped her reading or tidying or doing much of anything. Its being there had stopped anything coming to her. Maybe the umbrella the day before would not have been broken if she hadn't seen the fish just as she was reaching for it.

She forged a plan. She forged a plan to catch it. And when it was done? She was not certain. Fish stew or salted and left to dry till a dull day. Nothing got rid of a fish curse as well as a feast.

She'd caught fish before. That summer when something lopsided happened to the tides, storms every night and the spit-beach covered so often they couldn't get food to her for a week. She'd caught fish to feed herself; something wonderfully hysterical about holding on with her toes to the rock, gripping the rod. Never anything bigger than the piddly seaweed eaters who shoaled at the lighthouse base, stupid enough to bite onto nothing but the bare hook shine – but she could fish if she put her mind to it.

She decked herself out: the black slicker salt-wrecked round the cuffs and base; hat flaps clipped back; rough-handed gloves; green boots to the knee. There was something splendid about it: dressing up to fish.

Nothing the first day. Hours and hours of nothing but one wriggling usurper she threw back, disgusted. She stomped sorely inside and cooked, in a rage, the chicken she'd been saving for a special occasion.

Didn't bother with the costume the next day, only took the chicken bucket out in her bare feet and dungarees.

She caught a lot else with the gristle, threw some of them back, cut the rest into mouthfuls and put them on the hook to try the fish's tastes. Nothing. She kept her eyes open, dangled her extremities in to entice it – to make it think she had a message to give; gave up as disgruntled as before.

She womanned the radio all night without feeling tired at all, sluiced and scrubbed the walkway up top in the early light shift, mopped the lens on her tiptoes so the water ran down and onto her face. Later she tidied the book piles into alphabetical perfection, rearranged the cushions, put the shelves into systems.

In the morning, she heard the sound of the van driving down the straight rocky path that ran along the spit. Went out to meet it.

You busy? Lionel said, shifting forward.

Yeah. She took the first crate, upping it on her hip. She did not know why he always asked; she felt always busy: out every morning sifting for goods through the sands, scanning the water for something left behind. He didn't think magpie work amounted to much; he didn't know any better.

Not stormy though, Lionel said, not really, is it?

No. Not stormy, she said – though it had been.

They could say what they wanted about a woman lighthouse keeper. They could say anything they liked, and they would.

*　　*　　*

180

For a week she cooked up feasts that lasted her the radio-filled nights, sent carefully formed hellos to the lighthouse up the coast, where they didn't get the blusts half so bad. Coded jokes to the ships that locked onto her signal in their short passings. During the light shifts she read two books at once, swapping them page by page, made up crosswords to fill in when she forgot the clues; went through the clutter, tidying in her own way. Occasionally she went out with her rod and stood quiet, looking down for a silver snicker nosing up to the rocks. Had no better luck than before.

She'd been waiting for a day warm enough, and, when it came, danced out, tripped on the stairs, sent her collection of washing bottles rolling from her arms, and then stripped, yodelling, on the rocks directly at the base of the lighthouse. She fixed a thumb and finger round her nose, aimed, brought her knees up to her chest.

She felt the fish as she was swimming back up. It sent a thin lance of electricity through her leg and then another along her belly so she hit forward with mouth open and hands hunting to bring it head down onto the rock. She came up empty-handed, fingers opening and closing around air. Cooled her burnt belly on the stone, then turned to see the colour of the fish lilting away and down.

She washed: soaped everything twice, yarring at the knotted mass of hair till it hung out, sat thoughtful to let the clean soak in. Thinking on a fish.

The next time the tide eased, she got ready to go to town. Stood in front of the mirror and looked at the strangeness of herself. Made up from sea findings; the things left behind. It would be easy to never go anywhere. Leaving felt a feat, a heroic endeavour. She steeled herself: wellied up, walked over the rocks, down and along the beach into town.

At the Fords' boatyard Mr Ford was alone, sat on an overturned bucket, not doing much only looking. There were boats half painted and some were storm-broken or had been left to rot. There were seagulls resting or fighting for scraps.

I want to rent a boat, she said, just for a day.

He turned his face in her direction and moved his chin from side to side.

Too much, she said when he spoke and he turned his face back and forth and wrung his hands and said another number.

She watched his face, the way it settled after he spoke, and knew he was saying things silently to her, just as everyone in the town did.

When they were done she said: you'll take it down to the water for me? And the price rose again, dipped and rose and was settled on.

She liked the boat, its sturdy lines, the way it nodded obligingly when she settled at the motor end, arranging the sandwiches and the rod and the much-mended net in the bottom. Some of the men on the dock waved and even their waves meant something about a woman living alone in a lighthouse. She raised her finger to test the wind then turned it towards them, though they didn't seem to notice. Some days, she thought, she invented whole battles, whole wars which nobody else understood. Other days she was certain that the way a man picked up his pint glass meant something, the way a child dug in the sand or a woman hung out her washing. Everything was a threat, or promise, or a joke aimed loud enough in her direction she'd be certain to hear it.

She rode the boat until the shore was only a kind of line, and the lighthouse some sort of punctuated after-thought – an exclamation mark perhaps.

She tried a number of places that she knew were good from watching the fishing boats; docked the engine and settled back with her boots on the side and the rod running between them. What she caught was different from anything she'd ever hitched out from the side of the lighthouse, brighter and with bigger ideas. Most she threw back. They were not what she was looking for.

She sat there through the whole light shift. Ate her sandwiches one-handed, gutted some of the bigger fish and spread their innards on the water lid to call down to her fish, watched the big boats hauling in, each eye of their nets pupilled with a half-living silver thing, bucking and moaning. She waited longer than she ought, the sky darkening towards her, then reeled in and sat back to move the rudder.

The boat's narrow nose turning, she saw, barely in time, the slick of something at her elbow, bent to look. The fish's belly coming topside, rolling the way it had that first day. She did not reach for the net or move towards one of the hooks she could have driven down, only put her hand into the water.

The fish snickered under, back-flipping, rose again, laid its side along the bone of her wrist. She felt – though her teeth were clenched for it – no jut of electricity. Then the fish went low, gone.

She understood everything, pacing the small rooms, walking the circle of the walkway up top, the thought of the years the fish had lived taking any want to sleep from her. The hours loomed into one another; she invented histories: its birth in the shallows of a river; its forced tries at life there, the gulping up of stones to suck from the river base; its journey downstream until the water salted, until it felt the waves. It was only later – two bottles of wine from Lionel's delivery gone, and her saying everything she was thinking out loud – that she thought maybe everything she'd guessed about the fish was wrong; that it was, rather, a sort of metamorphosis. She went down to the slick rocks, drunk enough now to cry or laugh or fall in, and yelled her knowledge of the creature out into the cold foam. The way it could have stung her and did not; the way it moved with an almost human intelligence. Not a food source or a pretty thing to watch but, maybe, a friend.

In the morning she remembered only snapshots of thoughts, her mouth sanded thick, eyes gummed. She woke herself properly in the sea, and knew then that the fish was the same as her. She would not catch or eat it; she would protect it if she could.

There was money in places all over, taped to the underside of chairs and tables, shoved deep under the mattress, single notes shuffled away between the pages of books. She gathered it without much logic, remembering another place and dashing off. She imagined Bovary was marked with her well-worn pathways. The radio spasmed something out: a joke about tide lines or wind direction. She let the dial go down with a click till it was off, put on her wellies and shoved a handful of notes down the sides of them just in case, carrying the rest in the old satchel. She was too excited to worry much about town, about the people or anything else.

At the yard Mr Ford and Leo stood, headless, beneath an overturned and hoisted-up boat, working on the innards. She whistled them out.

Remember the boat you rented me? she said. I want to keep it longer. I want to keep it for a while.

The old man wiped oil from his fingers onto his chin in mock thought, worked the price till he was sweating and she was numb with rage and excitement. In the end, with them watching, she had to stick a fist into her left welly and pull out a handful.

She started away from them, swinging her arms, and then turned, came back. They had not moved any, were watching her return.

You got anything to drink?

The old man seemed to think about it for a long while. Went inside and came back carrying a bottle. There was no label on it and he had no glasses with him, but after he'd drunk she took it, swung it up. The boy had some too, eyes bulging round the rim. She stood. She wanted them to ask, that was it.

Have another, shall we? she said, and took it from the boy's hand and raised it again, closing her eyes into the tilt, passing it to the old man.

I'm celebrating.

She initiated the third round of the bottle, feeling a little shaky at the pressure of the words coming out, at the waxy sheen of their faces looking. She spun on her heel and took off away, almost losing her footing, and then, at a sound, looking over her shoulder at them –

What?

What you celebrating? the boy repeated, his father's face turning slowly from her to him and back again.

She thought about it. She wanted to explain everything to them. She wanted to tell them she'd had a mind to catch it but now she needed the boat only to watch it, to be near it. She did not have the words for that much. Only drew the silence out, knew it a mistake before it came, but drew, anyway, the silence out into words: I'm celebrating a fish.

* * *

Most days she took the boat out, stripped off her clothes, shrieking for the September cold, and jumped in, pretending there was no need for lungs until there was, feeling the fish mouthing about her like something laughing. Other days, she brought out tastes to try on it, dropping in the scatterings of steak or pitta bread and watching the pursed lips break the surface.

She cooked the feasts in the dark shift – the radio only half-womanned, the beam dusty – and then carted out the leftovers in the morning. She felt she could get used to anything, and did: the force of the cold and of drying in cold air; the salt that crusted her hair; the weight of sleeping barely hours or not at all; the days when the fish did not show, and she, thinking the worst, sat rocking and looked to the frothing nets of the nearby boats for a long shape. There was no knowing where it went in the hours without her. Some dark shifts, turning the radio to barely a hum, she wished she was the type to go, sit in the pub. She was not and besides: there was the light-house. Whose needs were so basic and childlike she did them as thoughtlessly as she did her own – it had never seemed like something hanging round her neck until now; weighted, bawling.

She was out hunting cockles when the truck came bouncing down the spit-path, throwing up clods of damp brought up from the beach. She straightened with hands on hips, said: I'm not due a delivery.

I left some stuff off your last. Thought I'd drop them by, Lionel said, and cocked his open mouth at her. He was thin with a paunch and a slouch and a give in his body and a face smooth as a child's.

There were two other people in the cab of the truck. The boy leant out on the bone of his arm; the girl very still, staring straight out the windscreen at her.

Kind of you, she said, and took the crate from him, felt, for a moment, the pressure of his hands holding on.

On the way to the truck he called: heard about your fish.

The girl made a low sound and the boy beat the butt of his fist against the metal and then withdrew. They reversed, turned at the end of the spit and started back towards town. She stood looking after it until it was gone.

When the tide was out she dragged the boat off the rocks, onto the beach and then pushed it out until it was deep enough to ride. When she came to the fish it was sculling the surface, lipping up at her when she leant towards it. Not far away one of the oil-slicked fishing boats was again pulling in great tides of dead and she sat and watched: the smeared bodies moving around the deck; the faces always turned in her direction. She did not strip her clothes off to swim – pulled the boat's anchor up long before the sky was darkening, turned towards home. The fish swam alongside her for a while and then fell back and down, like something shot.

That dark shift, she took a blanket up top and walked round and round, looking out. Shapes and shadows and the somethings the beam picked out looked like armies growing from the sands or snorkelled heads rising from the water. In the dying hours of the shift, there were explosions of sound and colour from the spit-beach – red and yellow sparks that went up and then came back towards the beach. Kids and firecrackers maybe, but she put it down as a warning.

The next day she decided she would not go looking for the fish. The sea was flat as a rock face and busy for it. There were more boats than normal, some fishing and others seeming only to float without occupation. On the beach, dogs ran, streaking beneath the heavy rain; sodden couples stood looking out at the indent of her lighthouse, waterproofed families trooped back and forth like sentinels.

As the light shift neared its end, she got ready to drag the marooned boat out to the wave line.

There were two trucks this time, juddering up and down over the rough, straight path, bumper to bumper, pulling to a stop in front of her where she stood next to the boat.

You forgot something else? she said.

Lionel sighed and twitched before her, jerking the back of his truck down to pull the bag forward. Sloppy work. Sloppy work, he said.

There were faces in both trucks looking out at her. She didn't take the time to count them. A dog came skittering down and barked at her. Lionel kicked it away with the toe of a boot.

I've got everything I need now, she said. I've got everything.

OK. He moved from foot to foot, tongue against the bridge of his lip. OK, OK. You going out in that boat? You going out in that boat there?

She shrugged.

Lionel walked away, sidling, kicking sand. He climbed in and the trucks jerked away. One of them leant on their horn until they were out of sight.

She stayed up top that afternoon. The sky was changing colour and looked, she thought, like something yawning up out of a place it had been stuck.

When she came out onto the stone ridge it was night and the beach was empty. The tide was out. She went to the boat and took a hold of the side and pressed her knee beneath its base to push it forward and then there was the sound, murmuring behind her, of a truck riding the beach.

She turned and watched it. It was pulling a dead weight behind it: a fishing boat, a hulking carriage wrecked and stained.

She saw easily, awfully, how this was only the first, that there were other vans, other boats behind. Yes, she could hear their rumble too now. They would catch the fish: most of them drunk, looping the net round twice to hold it firm, beating it once on the gunwale though this did little good, and that man sweating by the time the fish is

190

dead. There would be a measure of superstition after that: leaving it on the deck rather than putting it on ice, keeping their distance or going gamely close, while the others watched, to prod or kick it. They would take it to the pub. That would be the best place to show it to the rest, bringing it in above their heads, getting drinks for their troubles, taking it out to the kitchen and scoring the sides to let in the heat. Barely enough for a bite each and with the taste of marshes and fen earth, but more of a ritual than anything else, as potent as taking church bread onto your tongue.

Back inside she saw headlights pass through the windows, angling over the white walls. There were matches in one of the cupboard drawers, but she collated everything in her head before she struck one: leaning book towers and shards of material and everything else collected and ordered and known over the years. She could hear the rough breath of rutted wheels catching on damp sand; the sound of doors opening and closing. She scraped the match hard over the bridge of the box and turned it loose against the curtains. She did not stay to eye the burning of it or even think much on it as she humped the shallow edge of the boat across the last of the uncovered sand and then jerked a leg over. Behind her, in the dark, their echoing curses boomed like waves.

There was no way to know direction, a blind driving-off with only lights behind to tell her she was at least heading away: the beam of the lighthouse, and – soon –

the lesser, changing light of the flames through the windows.

She trailed the motor out to the right spot, let the anchor spool away, looked towards the shore, looked for the shape of the boats coming with intent towards her, but nothing there.

She pulled her socks off, stood somehow serenely balanced to remove trousers and T-shirt. She swam down, breath potent between her ribs. She lost light all the way down until it was dark enough only to feel the motion of something brushing at her leg.

ACKNOWLEDGEMENTS

THANK YOU TO:

Everyone at Eve White, particularly Jack Ramm.

Everyone at Jonathan Cape, most especially Alex Bowler.

All the readers: Sarvat Hasin, Kiran Millwood Hargrave, Tom de Freston, Susie Campbell, Gabby Penfold, Jess Oliver, Matt Bradshaw, Sam Thompson, Christine Lane and Becky Riddell.

All the Johnsons.